LIFE BEING THE BEST
& OTHER STORIES

A REVIVED MODERN CLASSIC

KAY BOYLE

LIFE BEING THE BEST & OTHER STORIES

Edited with an Introduction
by Sandra Whipple Spanier

A NEW DIRECTIONS BOOK

The contents of this selection of stories are taken from the earlier collections *Wedding Day and Other Stories* (1930), *The First Lover and Other Stories*
(1933), and *The White Horses of Vienna and Other Stories* (1936). Some of
the stories first appeared in the following magazines to which grateful ac-
knowledgment is made: *Contempo, Harper's Magazine, London Mercury, The
New Yorker, Scribner's Magazine* and *Spectator.*

Manufactured in the United States of America
First published clothbound and as New Directions Paperbook 654 in
1988
Published simultaneously in Canada by Penguin Books Canada Limited

Library of Congress Cataloging-in-Publication Data

Boyle, Kay, 1902–

Life being the best and other stories / by Kay Boyle ; edited with an
introduction by Sandra Whipple Spanier.
(A New Directions Book)
ISBN 0-8112-1052-9
ISBN 0-8112-1053-7 (pbk.)
I. Spanier, Sandra Whipple, 1951–   II. Title.
PS3503.09357L5 1988   87-32059
813'.52—dc 19   CIP

New Directions Books are published for James Laughlin
by New Directions Publishing Corporation
80 Eighth Avenue, New York 10011

CONTENTS

INTRODUCTION

When Kay Boyle's first book, a collection of short stories, was published in Paris in 1929, William Carlos Williams wrote: "Her short stories assault our sleep. They are of a high degree of excellence; for that reason they will not succeed in America, they are lost, damned. Simply, the person who has a comprehensive, if perhaps disturbing view of what takes place in the human understanding at moments of intense living, and puts it down in its proper shapes and color, is anathema to United Statesers and can have no standing with them. We are asleep."

He was only too accurate in his prediction of the commercial success of Kay Boyle's writing ("Surely excellence kills sales.") But she has never faltered in the bold articulation of her vision. In the course of her six-decade career, Kay Boyle has written over thirty-five books, including fourteen novels, eleven collections of short fiction, five volumes of poetry, two essay collections, and a memoir of Paris in the twenties. She has also translated three *avant-garde* French novels, ghostwritten two books, and edited several more volumes. Her first publication was a poem in Harriet Monroe's *Poetry*, when Boyle was in her teens, later followed by a number of others in that magazine. Hundreds of her stories, poems, and articles have since appeared in periodicals ranging from the "little magazines" published in Paris to the *Ladies' Home Journal* to *The Nation*. She has twice been awarded Guggenheim fellowships, won the O. Henry Award for best short story of the year in 1935 and again in 1941, holds a number of honorary degrees, and occupies the Henry James chair of the American Academy of Arts and Letters (one of only six women members of that select body of fifty writers, artists, and musicians). In 1981 she was awarded a Senior Fellowship for Literature from the National Endowment for the Arts for her "extraordinary contribution to contemporary American literature over a lifetime of creative work." And in 1987 she received an endowment from the Fund for Poetry "in support and appreciation of her contribution to contemporary poetry."

In 1978, the *San Francisco Chronicle* asked several contemporary writers for sketches of how they saw themselves. Kay Boyle's self-portrait was a line drawing of an angel in flight, complete with wings and halo, bearing a small round smoking bomb in each hand. Her caption reads, "Since receiving several volumes of censored data through the Freedom of Information Act, I see myself as a dangerous 'radical' (they themselves put it in quotes) cleverly disguised as a perfect lady. So I herewith blow my cover." (Her 2000-page FBI file contains a report that she had had an affair with Ezra Pound before World War I. "I would have been no more than ten," Boyle says. She did not meet Pound until 1927, in Paris, and she disliked him then.)

If outspoken political activism makes one a "radical," then probably the label fits. Since roughly the beginning of World War II, nearly everything Kay Boyle has written has been overtly political. Her 1944 novel *Avalanche* was the first book about the French Resistance (and, incidentally, her only bestseller). From 1946 to 1953, she was a foreign correspondent for *The New Yorker*, assigned to write articles and fiction on conditions in France, Spain, and Occupied Germany, until she and her diplomat husband, Joseph von Franckenstein—an Austrian baron who fled Nazism, became a U.S. citizen, and later was decorated for his heroic work with the OSS behind enemy lines—endured a McCarthy-style loyalty-security hearing. Despite their being cleared, Franckenstein was fired as "surplus," *The New Yorker* withdrew Kay Boyle's accreditation, and for the rest of the decade she found herself blacklisted. From the time she began teaching at San Francisco State University in 1963 and settled permanently in the United States, Kay Boyle has continued to voice her social and political concerns—protesting the war in Vietnam (and going to jail with Joan Baez and others for blocking the entrance to the Oakland Induction Center), participating in the student strike of 1968 (and getting herself publicly—but only temporarily—fired by university president S. I. Hayakawa), marching with California farm workers, founding a San Francisco chapter of Amnesty International, and continually speaking out on behalf of human rights around the globe.

Such are the signs of "radicalism" that a J. Edgar Hoover would recognize. What William Carlos Williams saw in her work and what these thirteen early stories represent is perhaps a less obvious but no less revolutionary approach to life and art. For Kay Boyle was in Paris in the twenties among the pioneers of modernism who called their aesthetic revolt "the Revolution of the Word."

Kay Boyle went to France in 1922 with her first husband, a French exchange student whom she met while he was studying engineering at the University of Cincinnati. Because by law at that time an American woman who married a foreigner automatically assumed her husband's citizenship, she was not technically an expatriate. But she was very much a part of the group of writers and artists that has since come to be known as the Lost Generation— a term she hates. Her friends included James Joyce, William Carlos Williams, Samuel Beckett, Hart Crane, Black Sun Press publishers Harry and Caresse Crosby, *This Quarter* editor Ernest Walsh (she left her husband to live with him in the South of France, and he was the father of her first child), and Robert McAlmon, that largely forgotten but enormously important figure of the Left Bank. At the time of his divorce from the poet Bryher (who wanted to be free to continue her relationship with H.D.), a generous settlement from his wealthy British father-in-law enabled McAlmon to found the Contact Press and to publish the first work of Ernest Hemingway and other young unknown writers, as well as that of Gertrude Stein.

But Kay Boyle's revolutionary training in the arts had begun long before she ever got to Paris, and her contacts with the *avant-garde* were not limited to writers. Alfred Stieglitz was a friend of her mother's, and from the age of eight or nine, Kay Boyle considered him a mentor. A show of children's art at his "291" Gallery included paintings by Kay Boyle and her sister. When her mother took her, aged eleven, to see the Armory Show in New York in 1913, Kay Boyle could hardly have imagined that in 1927 Francis Picabia would become the godfather of her first

child, that with Constantin Brancusi she would design a
carving for the marble crypt of that child's father, Ernest
Walsh (who died five months before his daughter was
born), that she would be photographed in Paris by Man
Ray, or that Marcel Duchamp would be a close friend and
the godfather of her sixth and last child, her son Ian, born
in 1943. (She describes Duchamp as a "wonderful man,
absolutely dauntless," and she dedicated *Avalanche* to
"Monsieur et Madame Rrose Sélavy"—Duchamp and
his longtime companion, Mary Reynolds. Reynolds was
active in the French Resistance and provided many details
for the novel; in turn Kay Boyle shared the profits from
the book with the couple.)

Kay Boyle's early poems and stories appeared in the
avant-garde magazines of the twenties alongside the work of
Ezra Pound, James Joyce, Gertrude Stein, William Carlos
Williams, Carl Sandburg, Djuna Barnes, and Ernest
Hemingway. Her contemporaries considered her one of
the most promising writers of their generation. Archibald
MacLeish declared in 1929, "She has the power and the
glory. I believe in her absolutely when she writes—even
when I want not to." In 1931 Katherine Anne Porter
wrote: "Gertrude Stein and James Joyce were and are the
glories of their time and some very portentous talents have
emerged from their shadows. Miss Boyle, one of the
newest, I believe to be among the strongest." William
Carlos Williams considered her Emily Dickinson's succes-
sor.

Of Paris in the 1920s, Kay Boyle has said, "all this
glorification of that wonderful Camelot period is absurd."
She firmly maintains that all those Americans were gathered in Paris mainly because of the favorable exchange

rate. The writers did not sit around in cafes and talk about
art. Most worked in isolation—many, including Kay
Boyle and her second husband, painter and surrealist
writer Laurence Vail, lived outside Paris or in the South of
France and visited the city only occasionally—and none
among them ever discussed their work. When she was with
James Joyce, he talked mainly about white wines and his
wife Nora talked about clothes. Had anyone mentioned
his writing, she claims, he would have got up and left the
table.

But if Kay Boyle debunks the legend of the Lost
Generation, she does not deny that a revolution was
taking place in Paris: "The recovery of the self was what
we were seeking in the twenties, although we never gave it
such a grand sounding name. Our daily revolt was against
literary pretentiousness, against weary, dreary rhetoric,
against out-worn literary conventions. We called our
protest 'the revolution of the word' and there is no doubt
that it was high time such a revolution take place. There
was *then*, before the twenties, no lively, wholly American,
grandly experimental, furiously disrespectful school of
writing, so we had to invent that school."

In 1929 Kay Boyle and Laurence Vail were among
sixteen writers and artists who signed a twelve-point
manifesto, written by Eugene Jolas and published in his
magazine *transition*, calling for the "Revolution of the
Word." It declared, among other things, "The writer
expresses. He does not communicate," and "The plain
reader be damned." Yet in the course of the thirties, living
in Austria, England, and France with Vail and their
children, she witnessed first hand the historical events
brewing toward cataclysm. By the time the family fled

war-torn Europe in 1941, she had come to the belief that the artist must not retreat into a heady solipsism, but must recognize a responsibility to communicate his or her fervent convictions to as many readers as possible— "plain" ones included. In most of her later work she takes as her material events of contemporary history and writes in a far more accessible style than earlier.

The stories in this volume—originally published in the collections *Wedding Day* (1930), *The First Lover* (1933), and *The White Horses of Vienna* (1936)—show an artist in transition. Some are products of her experience in Paris in the twenties and exhibit the idiosyncratic subject matter and complex, experimental style of the Revolution of the Word. In "I Can't Get Drunk," whose protagonist she later identified as Robert McAlmon, Boyle experiments with what the *transition* manifesto called the "language of hallucination," presenting a dialogue between a man and woman in a Paris bar through the woman's stream of consciousness. The disillusioned young woman of "Art Colony," trapped by poverty in a squalid commune of toga-clad *artistes*, is closely modeled on Kay Boyle herself, who after Ernest Walsh's death, lived with her infant daughter at the Neuilly colony of Raymond Duncan (Isadora's brother), whose followers wore togas and sandals and subsisted on yogurt and goat cheese. Like the woman in the story, Kay Boyle worked at the colony's gift shops—one on the Boulevard St. Germain and the other on the Rue de Faubourg St. Honoré—selling hand-woven tunics, hand-dyed scarves, and leather sandals to American tourists. She became disillusioned when Duncan (who delighted in introducing her as "the honey who drew the bees" to his shops) used the proceeds from his lectures on the virtues of the simple life to buy a luxurious American automobile. With the help of Robert McAlmon, she "kidnapped" her young daughter from the group and escaped the prison of the commune in late 1928.

But while Kay Boyle never loses sight of the personal struggle, other stories reflect a growing concern for matters of what she once called "the functioning world." In these stories the fate of the individual is inextricably bound up in larger political and social struggles. Kay Boyle delicately mocks the maiden fervor of three vacationing German sisters awaiting "The First Lover," but their eager expectancy takes on poignance when the attraction of the fine, fit Englishman is set so firmly in the context of their defeated nation's poverty and suffering: "They were in a new country of greed and plenty and they would forget, by turning their faces away, they would forget everything that made their hearts like winter apples."

Kay Boyle strove to write "with an alertness sharp as a blade and as relentless." (She wrote that Harry Crosby, who died in 1929 in a tragic suicide pact with a mistress he called the "Fire Princess," stood "singularly alone" in his "grave acknowledgement of that responsibility.") Typically in a Kay Boyle story, very little "happens." Her stories most often end not in resolution but in revelation— in a supercharged moment of truth that James Joyce would have called an "epiphany." Beneath the deceptively placid surface rushes a treacherous current that imperils our complacency. It is interesting how consistently reviewers and critics over the years have used metaphors of quiet disaster to describe Kay Boyle's work. An early reviewer wrote of her stories in the 1930s: "Here is poison—in the small doses in which arsenic is prescribed for anemia." In the 1980s, Margaret Atwood noted that while Kay Boyle's writing is sometimes spoken of as approaching the surreal, "there is nothing of the ant-covered clock about it": "One thinks rather of Breughel, a landscape clearly and vividly rendered, everything in its ordinary order, while Icarus falls to his death, scarcely noticed, off to the side."

Kay Boyle early gained a reputation as a brilliant stylist. Her skill is evident in her ability to fix an instant with photographic clarity or to animate a landscape as a reflection of the inner state of the perceiver. She captures with equal precision the voices of a drunken artist on a barstool, a jaded Italian surgeon about to perform his fourth mastoid of the day "and this one done in sterling," and a deceived but cleverly undaunted English lady who exacts her revenge on an insincere suitor in a series of impeccably correct epistles. Boyle is a master of the fresh, surprising metaphor, and she is capable of revealing character through complex internal monologues that rival those of Joyce and Faulkner in their psychological authenticity.

William Carlos Williams noted in Kay Boyle's work a distinctly female perspective. "Few women have written like this before," he said, "work equal in vigor to anything done by a man but with a twist that brings a new light into the whole Sahara of romanticism, a twist that carries the mind completely over until the male is not the seeing agent but the focus of the eye." Her work incorporates a wide swath of human experience simply relegated to invisibility in most fiction written by men. Her keen eye takes in the details of daily life that form the inevitable backdrop of existence for most women—"the vegetables, stiff as dead men on the table, waiting for water and fire to bring them life again," the slices of cold potato "browning sweetly in the butter." Her work reflects the experience of a woman who has raised eight children, six of her own and two from Laurence Vail's previous marriage to Peggy Guggenheim. She displays a keen ear for the voices of children, an aching concern for their vulnerability, and an astute and unsentimental observation of their ways. ("The stone hearts of little girls belonged, like those of perverts, in a privy world of their own," she writes in "Convalescence.")

Despite the surface diversity of her work, set anywhere from a Paris art colony to an English estate to the Australian outback, written in the "language of hallucination" or the language of the *Saturday Evening Post*, Kay Boyle's is a unified vision. F. Scott Fitzgerald claimed that in a lifetime a writer writes only two or three stories, over and over. Kay Boyle did not know Fitzgerald in Paris (she encountered him only once, in New York in 1922, when she and her sister went to see the young celebrity at a book signing at Columbia University, where he was surrounded by adoring autograph-seekers) but she probably would agree with the observation. At the heart of Kay Boyle's central story is a belief in the absolute essentiality of love—both on a private and a public scale—and a sense of tragic loss when human connections fail, leaving individuals who are desperately in need of contact bouncing off one another like atoms. The plight of the young man of "I Can't Get Drunk" is the plight of all lonely and isolated humanity: "To see him with his lean mouth closed like a wallet, his eye like iron and as cold as, would it ever have come into your head that the mouth of his heart was open, was gaping wide like a frog's in dry weather, requesting that into it be drained not glasses with frost on their faces but something else again." He is gasping for love like oxygen, not even knowing what he needs.

The plumber tells the astronomer's wife as he leads her away from her egotistical husband, "There's nothing at all that can't be done over for the caring." But with the exception of a few stories like "Astronomer's Wife" and "His Idea of a Mother" that end in a glimmer of hope for rescue, Kay Boyle's work explores the tragedy of love not lost but never gained. Kay Boyle is an idealist in her view of human possibilities but a pessimist about their chances for fulfillment.

Boyle's stories are a catalog of the ways in which love can fail. In some, connection is blocked by quirks of the individual psyche, by misunderstanding, by pride—and in the case of "The Meeting of the Stones" and "To the Pure," the problem is complicated by a conflict in sexual orientation. But in other stories in this volume and in much of Kay Boyle's later work, the barriers to contact are institutionalized and large scale; the forces keeping human beings apart are social, political, historical. In "Life Being the Best," the humanistic teachings of the gentle schoolmaster begin to transform the imagination of a motherless Italian boy whose family has taken refuge from Mussolini's black shirts in the South of France. "The words he used were never on anyone else's tongue in the country: such things as 'the might of thought,' and 'the power of the soul,' he spoke of, and undid Jesus from the cross and made a wounded weeping man of him." But Kay Boyle ultimately forces us to the tragic conclusion that in our time the simplest values of brotherly and sisterly love and respect for human life are no match for the crushing forces of militarism, poverty, and oppression.

Kay Boyle's world most often is a grim place. But it is not a meaningless Waste Land. In her youth, she and her companions burned T. S. Eliot and Ezra Pound in effigy on the Rue de Montparnasse. Then, as now, she had little patience for the high art of alienation and despair. She believes that there are still responsibilities to be taken, choices to be made. Her stories are mined with bitter ironies, but she is never ironic about her basic belief in the power of human compassion and understanding to transform the world. In Paris in the twenties and thirties, she has said, stories "were written in protest, and also in faith, and they were not unlike fervent prayers offered up for the salvation of man, for the defense of his high spirit, for the celebration of his integrity." The irony that pervades so much of her work is not the mark of cynicism but the scar of a betrayal of faith, of a deep disappointment in humanity's failure to live up to its infinite capacity.

—Sandra Whipple Spanier

LIFE BEING THE BEST
& OTHER STORIES

LIFE BEING THE BEST

The schoolteacher's name was Mr. Virgil: a lean, loving, scholarly young man who had no wife as yet. Whatever he had in care and passion went out to the altering natures of his pupils. He drove their thoughts from one thing to the next even as they themselves coerced the cattle piece by piece down the road in the evening; he burned uneasily in their hearts because of his pure exalted eye. They had no explanation for him, nor could they talk of him among themselves without shifting and smiling, because the words he used were never on anyone else's tongue in the country: such things as "the might of thought," and "the power of the soul," he spoke of, and undid Jesus from the cross and made a wounded weeping man of him. Whenever Mr. Virgil came out under the olive trees where the boys were playing they fell silent a moment as if a great man were passing by.

It was sweet for them to have such a man for a change, for he never lifted a hand to them. There were parents who had no patience with this and they made up for it at home. But no one could say that the boys were wilder this year than any other, and their lessons were better learned with him than with any man before him. Palavicini spoke the softest words of all for Mr. Vigil. He said, "This year my son is pleasant and kind, the way he was before my wife died."

On an early morning in June they might be seen, Mr. Virgil and Young Palavicini, walking up to the school-house together under the low, silvery boughs. The boy was thin and stained dark by the mountains, and his hair curled up black on his head, while Mr. Virgil had been laved pale by ablutions of learning, had been made a gaunt man of because of his pacings to and fro in the asylum of his mind. Over their heads the olives were taking shape, no more than green buttons finishing off each twig.

"All things are to be learned from books," Mr. Virgil was saying. "So you should have the patience to learn. All earthly," he began gently, but suddenly he must skip aside to avoid an island of cow-dung in the path, "and all unearthly things. Take care, don't soil your boots, Palavi-cini," he said, and with his hand on the boy's shoulder they walked on under the olive branches. "It gives you a certain kind of power to know many things."

This was the way they came to school together in the morning, and Mr. Virgil, with his open palm resting on the tree's flank, said, "A tree is armed by nature with its bark, and an enlightened man is armed with knowledge. Take Jupiter, for instance. Do you remember how he held the thunderbolt high in his right hand?"

But before Young Palavicini could speak of these things he must disguise and hush his voice with shyness so that no hidden ear might overhear and shame him.

"Or Jesus," he said hoarsely, "with his cross. Every time I've seen Jesus he had hold of it."

"No," said Mr. Virgil, gravely but sweetly, "that isn't the real meaning."

"Oh, yes, I'm sure," Young Palavicini said. "Oh, yes, I remember. That's why we left Italy, Chiesa's people and mine. After awhile everybody in Italy had to put a black shirt on or else Jesus came along and made trouble."

"No," said Mr. Virgil gently. "You must be thinking of someone else, Palavicini. Jesus lived a long time ago."

"Yes, yes," said the boy, "yes, I know. He was in jail once for socialism. There was a photograph of him being taken away by the *carabinieri*."

Mr. Virgil did not speak but reached his hand above his head and broke off a deadening branch from the tree. He took the knife from his pocket and opened the blade out with the nail of his thumb.

"Look here, Palavicini," he said, and he ran the black bark off under the knife's edge. There lay the drying wood revealed, stainless and white below. "Knowledge can do this thing to your mind," he said softly. "It can be like a sharp knife whittling your thoughts clean for you."

So he spoke of it, as though knowledge were a light that might suddenly be cast down in glory upon the hearts of children. But Young Palavicini stood still a long while, watching the stick come clean, with his own thoughts moving slothful and slow in his head.

"Think of when your papa goes hunting," said Mr. Virgil, and he looked softly and winningly into the boy's face. "Now what is the first thing he would take?"

He paused there in the fresh morning light and looked in hope and tenderness at Young Palavicini. But the boy could not force his thoughts to the answer, could not perceive what he was expected to say. After a little he said:

"First he would borrow the umbrella from Chiesa's people," and the light of pleasure died in Mr. Virgil's face.

"No, no," said the schoolmaster quickly. "Now let us think about it." He lifted his head, as though the gift and rhapsody must come from elsewhere and purify his tongue lest he speak out of the bigotry of man toward child. "Let us think of your papa going hunting," he said. "He is going out after partridge or after hare."

"Chiesa runs like a hare if you turn on him," said Young Palavicini, and the corners of his mouth went down as if the taste were bad.

"Ah, don't speak ill of the other boys!" said Mr. Virgil sadly. "Chiesa should be close as a brother to you. You came from the same country at the same time, mothers and fathers together."

"Have you seen how he runs with his toes out?" said Young Palavicini, the words falling fast from his mouth. "Have you seen the smile on his face, and the dirt on his neck, and the tongue hanging out when he stands at the window watching," until Mr. Virgil clapped his hands over his ears and cried out:

"I've heard enough, Palavicini! We were speaking of your papa going off into the woods. What is it he takes with him, carried over his shoulder?"

The two of them halted now and stood silent, looking into each other's face as they stood on the whitish grass. Down behind went the low hills, and the orchards and the vineyards of the country, wan and pale with the shallow greens and lemons of the south. Mr. Virgil's lips were parted now and a tentacle of hope was reaching across his features; but the little boy stood speechless and seemingly thoughtless, with his eyes gone black and ignorant in his face.

In a little while Young Palavicini said, "I don't know."

"But of course your papa would take his *gun*!" cried Mr. Virgil, laughing. "Don't you see? If he's going out hunting he takes his gun, and when he hears a sound or a rustle of life," said the schoolmaster warily, "he takes aim like this," and here he fell upon one knee and lifted the whittled olive branch to his shoulder. "He takes aim, like this, and then when the bird or the animal comes out he pulls the trigger and lets the bullet fly."

"Oh, yes," said Young Palavicini, watching Mr. Virgil get to his feet again.

"That's the way knowledge can be used," said the schoolmaster, brushing the white dust of the soil from his knees. A few more steps and they had come to the threshold of the schoolhouse. There Mr. Virgil put the key in the lock of the door. "Just as bullets fly from the gun," said the schoolmaster gently, "so you can let powerful words spring from your tongue and serve as deadly weapons."

He pushed the door open and they walked in, submerged at once in the lake of swimming light within the room. Mr. Virgil stepped onto the platform that held his desk on high, and his hands ran over the papers, settling edge to edge in order the sheets of tall childish lettering the boys had written in strong purple ink. Young Palavicini sat on the bench below and crossed his hands on his knees.

"God came in and cried all night, Mr. Virgil," he said, "the time my mother died."

"No," said the schoolmaster gently, sorting the papers from one side to the other in his hands. "No, it must have been somebody else, Palavicini." He did not lift his eyes from the work on his desk before him.

"Yes, he was wearing a black dress," said Young Palavicini. "But when he went out in the garden he took his skirt to the one side and did it standing up the way a man does. And afterwards he got drunk when he was crying and he fell under the table and he and papa slept all night on the floor. I remember it. God wouldn't go home until he had his beads back out of the bottle where they had fallen into, and they couldn't get the beads out until they had finished the bottle."

Suddenly Mr. Virgil stepped down from the platform and walked around the end of the bench, and there sat down beside the little boy. He sat close to him on the wood, on the thick pewlike timber that was polished high by the impatience of young backsides shifting for a good sight out the window. He put his scholarly hand on the little boy's brow and his fingers drew back the dark loose hair. There he sat close to him on the form, with his arm about him, soft as a mother might do.

He said, "God is not a man," and his voice was sorrowful in his mouth. "He passes through all things and through the flesh even, but unseen, and always unharmed."

The little boy, held close against the schoolmaster's ribs, shook his head at these words.

"No," he said, "I saw him. He had a sore toe from coming so far that night, and my sister put brandy on it. He had a round blue mark, sitting like a crown in the middle of his hair."

When he came home from school in the evening he would take the skins off the vegetables in haste and fling them into the pot of water on the coals, scarcely taking the carrots' hides off, or the dirt, for all the hate he had in him for the work he was doing. There was a glass in the room that gave him a sight of his own face; but what was there in it but a well of fury for all the things to be done, the storm of the eyes gathering black in the firmament, the teeth shining white as tapers?

The lane between the two rows of houses was still, for the other boys played out on the square where the high-road passed and elegant cars went by from better places. From the window he could hear their voices calling and even taste the veil of dust that moved forth, as if borne from the highway and laid over the light walls of the street. Whenever it was a lorry that passed instead, he knew it by the dishes quaking on the shelf and the smell of castor oil left hanging in the air. He stood at the window, listening to the boys beyond, and he himself given in anger to the evening meal, captive, like any old woman in her kitchen.

In this window and out the door the wind had blasted, sucking grandmother, and then the aunt, and last the mother out, rattling them, bone and skin, one by one out the doorway. The thoughts in his head were of the room of death in the house that was closed now against the current of air that swept through it. One year it was the first, and the next the other who went out the door, and now there was only one woman left: there was the sister left to come walking down over the cobbles in the evening, stepping high on her angular heels from bucking stone to stone.

The lane was still, but he knew that in a little while the boys would be returning. He carried the tin pitchers out in his hands, and he lingered by the fountain in the soft, failing hour, dividing the water's strong flow in his fingers, as the mesh of a stout rope might be undone and done again. In a while he brought the pitchers back, slopping over with water, leaving a trail of black pursuant steps behind him on the cobbles as he came. He stood for a moment at the door, harking to the voices of Chiesa and the others on the square, standing alone but turning his thoughts of loneliness aside, like stray sheep turned to the shelter of Mr. Virgil's fold.

Chiesa was the first to return down the lane, skipping from side to side of it. His hair was cut close on his skull and his face was bleached by the platters of spaghetti and sauce that were always set before him. When he saw Young Palavicini on the step he jumped sideways to his own door.

"Hello," said Young Palavicini, scarcely speaking aloud.

"Hello," said Chiesa, with his lip drawn smartly back.

Young Palavicini looked shyly across at Chiesa on the other side.

"What makes of cars was it drove by this evening?" he said faintly.

"What's that to you?" said Chiesa, and his tongue ran out through his teeth in scorn. "Cooks," he said, "should keep their noses in their kitchens."

He skipped into the house at this, stamping his heels like a slippery hare in flight. Young Palavicini leaned down for the pitchers of spring water and bore them into the house in silence. But there he halted before the mirror and eyed the dark boy there with burning glance to glance.

Now he could no longer woo or bend his thoughts, and

up the stony flights of fury leaped the wild scattered flock. He could hear the cries from their bleating mouths as they went past him, and the slip of their hoofs seeking foothold in the treacherous shale. Once they had reached the top, he knew they would turn on themselves and swoop down in terror upon him, and he could not head them elsewhere. Whatever weapons of speech Mr. Virgil might have whittled for him, the wild fire of his anger would have taken them for kindling now.

What do you find in him to hold against him? he could hear Mr. Virgil's far voice complaining. But the flames of his rage snapped up berry and bush, and sent the sparks crackling to heaven. The dark trees of Mr. Virgil's patience shriveled and writhed in their burning needles and spat out their juices on the fiery forest moss. Have you seen how his hair grows, how his ears stand out, how he skips, sidles, shifts?—came the furious pack cantering, cantering in rhythm over the smoldering ground. Have you seen the seat of his pants, the back of his neck, the green in his eye, his mouth twisting up when a question's put, his velvet on Sunday, the tail off his cat, have you seen him cleaning his teeth with his fingernail? Down swept the pack with the fire licking behind them, driving them thirsting and frenzied against the scorching vineyard wall. There the clamor of their soft hot feet gone mad for succor stampeded Young Palavicini under. Have you seen how he eats, drinks, jumps, whistles, owns the best cars passing, spits, swings, screams laughing, tears, lies, blows his nose in his apron, sucks his spaghetti, cries, strikes, have you seen it, Mr. Virgil, have you seen it, have you seen it? . . .

So he was standing, holding to the chair for support,

staring still into the glass in anguish when his sister came home from the city store.

"Is the soup on yet?" she said first in the summer darkness; and Young Palavicini said, "Yes, the supper is on," scarcely able to speak from the fury that had spent him. She had walked into the fading room again and caught him at it, like any other evening caught him before the glass, iron eye to eye, storming. She might even see through to the thoughts of his head, see his temper swooning now in his blood. But instead she sat down on a chair with her hat on the back of her head. She was dressed like an idle lady, in imitation of the idle ladies her poverty served.

"I'm tired, I'm tired," she said, so gently that the whole darkening room crept suddenly into her lap and burst out crying.

"I'm tired," she said, and the light from the street came softly into the room, as Mr. Virgil might, and set back the hair from her forehead. "I'll make an omelette in a minute," she said. "I'll put something together for a change. I'll see you eat proper."

But by this time the room of itself was nodding, sleeping, snoring.

"I'll feed you up," said his sister, with the room rocked soft in her arms. Young Palavicini stood quiet by the window. Her legs had fallen apart and lay like dead men in her skirts. "In just a minute," she said. "In just a minute."

He saw the lamplight spring up in the windows of Chiesa's house, and the brothers and sisters there sit down to supper at the table. The mother moved from place to place, as his mother had done, setting the full plates of food before them. He could see Chiesa's black apron buttoned up to the back of his neck, and the movement of his jaw on his food as he bowed his shaved head and ate.

By Thursday a floating, spinning fog had settled deep on the hills, but Mr. Virgil had said they would walk to the monastery together whatever the weather might be. The two of them set out early, with their bread and their cheese in their pockets, and the obscurity bound fast as white silk on their eyes. If the schoolmaster had not known the way so well, they might have mistaken it even at the outset when they were still climbing warily through the stems of the young black pines. But he knew the curve and the feature of every branch as if they were human faces, and he knew very well how the path took its ease across the foothills.

"If it starts in to rain, it will be a good thing," said Mr. Virgil, "for the rain will clear the mist away."

The path led them up and on, but there was no sense of toil or climbing; except for the breath running hard in their bodies, they might have believed they were walking on level ground. The maquis and the heavy boulders of the country were veiled from sight, and it was only through memory they knew that a great valley was now opening out to the side. To Young Palavicini it seemed the air came fresher here: whether it was that he knew in his mind how the river's valley lay deep and wide below, or whether for the sight of the mist taking shape on the unseen edge and falling, wraith by wraith, into the seething vapors of the vacant place.

Here they breathed deeply, but there was no sign of the smoke from their mouths on the air; and Mr. Virgil said:

"If life is the best of all good things, Palavicini, then what would the worst of all evils be?"

But just as he spoke the call of a bird rang out from the invisible trees, calling "Cuckoo," tentatively, far but clear. The schoolmaster lifted his head in pleasure and, looking toward Young Palavicini, he laid his finger on his own lips. The boy could see the sound taking shape slowly in Mr. Virgil's lean long throat. And then "Cuckoo!" pronounced the schoolmaster in answer, calling out the same clear wondrous sound. It might have been no more than a drop of water falling into hollowness, the bird's tongue uttering, and then the schoolmaster's voice like an echo in return.

There was a little while of silence while they waited, and the forms in the mist went hastening, writhing by. And again the voice of the bird called out, but now quite near to them, speaking out in soft misgiving, "Cuckoo!"

Even the ordinary sound of Mr. Virgil's conversation did not affright the unseen bird, but it pursued them as they walked, following from branch to branch the clear word spoken in imitation on the schoolmaster's tongue. All sight was masked in blowing shrouds about them, but at intervals as he talked Mr. Virgil raised his head and called out the single word, drawing the bird after them in hope, "Cuckoo! Cuckoo!" like a pearl held captive on a silver chain.

"Life being the best of all good things," the schoolmaster was saying, "then what would follow as the worst of all evils?" And here he paused to answer the bird's troubled question. "Cuckoo!" he said lightly in reply.

"Would school be the worst?" said the boy in his soft modest voice. He was seeking to climb easily in the man's unflagging stride.

"Ah, no," said the schoolmaster gently, but there was sorrow in his face as well. "Ah, no. Don't you see that the worst of all things would be any action that takes life away?"

The bird's sweet wooing voice spoke hesitantly again, asking some avowal of the speechless mist; and now Mr. Virgil spoke out in warmth and promise, "Cuckoo, cuckoo, cuckoo!"

"Death," said the schoolmaster, "is a great robbery, Palavicini. It takes the sight from the eyes, the words from the mouth, the breath from the nostrils. Think about it," he said, "consider it. Perhaps that would be good as the theme for composition this coming week. 'Life Being the Best of All Good Things, Then Murder'—or let us say homicide—'Then Homicide Is the Worst of All Evils.'"

As the bird cried out its sad, strange note again, Young Palavicini said, "What is homicide?"

"The act of dealing death to another," said Mr. Virgil. "Cuckoo!" he called out with fervor. "You remember the story of Cain and Abel. When one man kills another, Palavicini, that is homicide."

The altering scale of the bird's question came wondering, querying, troubled, on the air. But now Mr. Virgil had no ears for it. He had halted on the perilous high path and turned to face the boy over the clear separate place their two bodies hollowed in the fog.

"Yes," he said ardently, "it will do you all good to write out such argument. It will make things clear for your own eyes, just as God might breathe upon it now and blow this mist away. You are all so different, you boys," said Mr. Virgil, "so that each of your declarations will be different. You and Chiesa, for instance, as different as two boys could be."

But suddenly the bitter taste of that name came cold in the little boy's mouth.

"Chiesa. I hate Chiesa," he said.

"No," said the schoolmaster strongly, "I do not believe it." He laid his arm over Young Palavicini's shoulders, and he said, "We will talk of this theme as we go on together." But the bird, calling out in concern for its love's direction, interrupted them again.

"Cuckoo!" said the bird, speaking low and clear from the forest.

"Cuckoo! Cuckoo!" Mr. Virgil turned his head and said.

It was almost noonday when the walls of the monastery stood forth from the mist, and the trees, lying newly felled near the path, were visible on the ground. The place had been left to fall to ruin for many years past, but the archway that rose before them was still unbroken, wide and high, with seats struck under its shelter out of the powerful stone. A dozen men riding abreast might have passed through it with ease were it not for the dark ivy that now would catch in their hair.

The courtyard within was ankle-deep with soft wet muck, a black stubborn despair that sucked at their boots and clung fast to their soles beneath them as they crossed. It was a great open court, with the floor of it done over and over with the marks of goats' hoofs; mist hung like curtains at the ends of the mighty place, but the center was cleared away as if for dancing. The bird did not follow them here, having come so far after them, but was left calling out endlessly with its ear cocked for answer in the muffled forest behind.

When the schoolmaster and the little boy walked into

the court, a window came open in the monks' habitation, and a woman leaned out and spoke in greeting.

"Well, then, here I am again!" Mr. Virgil called out in a high, gay voice, and two lean dogs came wailing down the worn-out stone. The schoolmaster took off his hat to her, and his short hair stood up in disorder against the heavy weather. She was a plump, dark-eyed woman, and dimples ran into her cheeks when she smiled.

Mr. Virgil stood tall as a tree in the courtyard, and the two dogs smelled back and forth across his shoes. The woman closed the window, and in a moment she came to the doorway with a shawl laid over her shoulders, and the dogs moved uneasily, in suspicion of Mr. Virgil and the boy.

"Come in," said the woman. "Come in. You must be wet to your skins in this weather."

The faces of the two young children at her skirts did not alter when one dog lifted his hind leg and quietly watered Mr. Virgil's leg. The schoolmaster was looking straight into the woman's face and he took no notice either.

"Here's one of my best lads I've brought with me," said Mr. Virgil, and he dropped his hand in love on Young Palavicini's shoulders.

"He's a beautiful child," said the woman. They mounted the steps together and he shook her dark soft hand.

Here in the room there was a great fire burning, for this was the old-time eating place of the religious men. The schoolmaster hung his cloak by the side of the flames, and there it was shining and dripping at once from the weight of soaking mist it had borne. The chimney was so large and tall that the woman bade Young Palavicini to step inside it and sit down on the stool in the corner. This he did, and put out his wet boots to the fire, but the woman said, speaking now in Italian to him:

"You'll be getting chilblains on your feet. Take your boots off and set your stockings aside."

But Young Palavicini could not bear to take off his boots before her, nor before the schoolmaster, nor before the young children who stood gazing at the sight of him there. Once his foot was out of his shoe they would see the state of his stockings. Mr. Virgil sat down at his ease, and pointed out the carving on the stones about them.

"Take off your shoes then," said Mr. Virgil, but Young Palavicini sat silent. In a moment the woman came back and set down a loaf on the table, and when she saw the boy sitting so, shamed by the fire, she stepped onto the hearthstones herself and knelt down.

"Here, let me have your feet," she said, and she ran her fingers under the lacings. "I've a son of my own as big as you," she said. From where she knelt by the burning wood she looked up at him, smiling; her eyes were bright as coals, and her cheeks blushing from the flame.

"Where's the husband and the son today?" said Mr. Virgil.

"They're out with the goats," she said, rising. She took the blackened kettle off the irons and poured the water from it into a copper pan. "I can give you butter and fresh cheese and cherries at once," she said to the schoolmaster as she knelt again. "But for warm milk, you'll have to wait till the goats come in."

"Ah, we've brought enough food along to keep us," said Mr. Virgil. He sat watching her dip the boy's red feet into the pan of water and he said, "I'm afraid there may be trouble, Mrs. Marincola, about the trees that you've taken down."

"I've washed my feet already this week," said the boy, but the woman gave no sign of hearing, but rubbed the soap well into his shining flesh.

"If there's anything said," the woman began, with a shadow fallen on her.

"It won't come from me," said Mr. Virgil, smiling.

"No," said Mrs. Marincola. "I'm sure of that." She took Young Palavicini's feet into the apron on her lap, and she said, "How is it there're such great holes in his stockings?"

"He's a good boy, Palavicini," said the schoolmaster quickly. "He takes care of his own house as well as a woman might. He gets home from school in time to start the supper for his father and his sister. His father's a mason, and his sister works in a shop in the city. His mother died of the influenza a year and a half ago."

The woman took the boy's feet close in her hands.

"I want *her* son to come to the schoolhouse too," said Mr. Virgil, smiling at Young Palavicini.

"We live too far from it," said Mrs. Marincola , and she chafed the boy's feet in the palms of her hands.

"I've told you before, if he can go out all day on the hills with the goats, he can come as far as the schoolhouse," said Mr. Virgil.

"How could he get home in the night?" said the woman. "He couldn't come so far alone."

"You've no right to keep your son away from school," said Mr. Virgil sternly.

"Listen," said Mrs. Marincola, speaking with the boy's feet pressed close in the soft bosom of her dress. "I've told

you too how it was when we came from Italy. We tried to
live in town then, and you know how hard it was, Mr.
Virgil, with the language to learn, and the working papers
you can't get for money or anything. You know very well
how my husband was almost a year without working."

"Yes," said the schoolmaster, and he sat nodding his
head and looking far away into the flame.

"I told you how we had to live some way or another,"
she said, "and here was this monastery crying for habitation. Now we have money put aside with the goats we
have, three hundred now, Mr. Virgil. If there's anything
said about the trees we can pay whatever it is they're
worth."

"Yes," said Mr. Virgil. "Yes, yes, I know."

They had no more than finished the lunch she set out
for them on the table, than a great murmuring of life arose
from the courtyard or from the forest beyond. A great
music of bells and of voices bleating came crowding and
pressing through the windows.

"There are the goats," said the woman, and she jumped
up to clear off the table. Young Palavicini, in the other
boy's sheepskin slippers, went shyly out the door to see.

The goats had just begun to enter the courtyard, coming
one by one, separately and tentatively, with heads lifted,
stepping warily and choosing their direction, as if bringing
the others behind them to safety at last. Outside the arch
the mist stood close, seemingly sealed against the stone's
open mouth, but still the flock of goats took shape in it,
hoof by hoof, near to the ground only, as a curtain would
stir and show the feet of many little dancers below its hem.

One after another the shy beasts came, speaking one

another's names uncertainly in sweet bewildered tones. They came stepping over the black soft muck with their long coats hanging coarse and clean and the bells at their throats ringing clearly. But when they saw the boy and the schoolmaster standing on the step they threw up their heads and set to charging wildly around the courtyard's rim. One look from the ends of their yellow eyes was enough to send them cavorting in fright and pleasure the length of the monks' forsaken yard.

In poured the goats, faster and faster through the archway, some as white as angels, and some bearing horns as long as the boy's arm. In the center of all the tumult, the great he-goats paired and locked their mighty cornucopias together, buckled and smote each other's weapons, pressed in their fury brow to brow. The goatlings ran by their mothers' sides, weeping, their own little horns no bigger than toadstools on their heads.

In a while the three hundred beasts were herded into the courtyard, and then came the man and his son, with their blankets and sticks, and their shepherd's capes on them, walking dark and hooded out of the deepening mist. Young Palavicini stood by the door even after the others had entered, listening to the Italian words that passed among them. The young children kissed their father's face and kissed their brother, and the woman went from one to the other, bearing their wet things away. Mr. Virgil cast a new log onto the fire, bringing it with difficulty, for all his strength, from the corner of the room to the chimney's blackened floor. When the big boy had drawn a pail of milk from the goats' bags they all drank of it, sitting at the table with the cheese and the bread and the cherries set out afresh as they had been before.

But when Mr. Virgil saw that Young Palavicini was not among them, he walked out to the doorway and drew him in.

"Come in, come in," he said. "We've a long way to go and you must warm yourself through before we start."

There they all sat at the round table, speaking of many things; but the schoolmaster did not bring up the question of school again, perhaps because of the uselessness of it, or perhaps because of the shadow of grievance it would cause to fall upon their faces. The woman was drawing her needle and the black wool in and out through Young Palavicini's stocking, mending it whole over her hand as she talked or gave ear to her husband's laughter.

The son sat near to Young Palavicini, and in a while he leaned over and set the plate of dark cherries and a tin cup of goat's milk before him.

"This is for you," he said, and his own teeth were stained black with the fruit.

"All these?" said Young Palavicini.

"Yes," said the other one, "yes, all."

They sat close to each other, with their backs going hot at the fire, so close that Young Palavicini could smell the strong odor of beasts and rain that dried on the other's coat.

"You may keep my sheepskin slippers," said Young Marincola, with his voice scarcely heard above the talk of the older people.

"To take home?" said Young Palavicini, but he did not turn his head.

"Yes," said the other, "to take home when you go."

After a little the father began singing to them. The bottle of red wine had turned to beauty in his blood, and he flung up his head and tossed back the black hair that fell across his brow.

"Oh, Italy, my fairest dove, your wings shall rise again!" he sang, and his voice shook loud and loving against the solemn stone. His face was round and rich with health, and his teeth as white as a dog's teeth in his mouth. From his short dark neck, loud enough to make a boy hide his face in shame, there rose in fervor this wondrous tide of sound.

"Oh, every child of Italy, save courage for the day when, galley slaves no longer, we will cast the chains away!" he sang, until the tears ran down the woman's face and she wiped them off with the back of her hand. When Young Palavicini looked at the Marincolas he felt the breath come short in his own heart.

Suddenly the woman turned her soft face to Young Palavicini, and she said:

"What kind of a life has this poor one now with no one to look out for him? He should be with his own people, coming from the same part of the country."

But Mr. Virgil stood up, laughing.

"You don't want to take one of my best lads from me, do you, Mrs. Marincola?" he said, shaking his head in jest at the woman. But now he fastened his cloak under his chin, for the hour had come for them to go. The woman put the warm stockings back on Young Palavicini's feet again and buttoned his jacket over.

"You will bring him again, Mr. Virgil?" she said, and she kissed the two sides of the boy's face.

"Yes," said the schoolmaster, "for I will come every week, either the Thursday or the Sunday, until you let your boy come to the schoolhouse as well."

The husband went down the steps before them, leading them through the cold precipitant bodies of the goats lying in the courtyard; he came as far as the archway, and then the schoolmaster and the little boy went on alone down the covert hill.

Near sunset the change in the day took the fog off with it, and the valley was drained clear with twilight as they came walking home. They came down through the olive orchards and the vineyards; and the tree trunks, and the rocks, and now the roofs beginning stood sharp and single as if coming forth refreshed from rest. They did not speak for peace and contentment, but descended thinking of how the day had passed. But when they came to the highroad above the town, it seemed a long smooth beach on which the tides of silence must break at last.

The other boys were still playing out on the square, and the sound of their voices traveled high and far. But as if to save himself the sight of them, Mr. Virgil halted before they came to the center of the town and put out his hand to Young Palavicini.

"Life Being the Best of All Good Things," he said softly. "Keep it in mind, Palavicini." He took the boy's hand in his and he said, "Good night. I'm going home this way. We'll meet in school tomorrow."

Young Palavicini stood silent, holding to the schoolmaster's hand. And thank you, my God, my Love, said his heart, but his lips would have none of it. Keep me now from going home to that face in the glass, cried his sorrow, but his mouth would not utter. Instead he stood staring wildly into Mr. Virgil's magic hand. He could see how the lines coursed this way and that on it, but he could not speak out his love for their directions. Instead he said:

"Good night, Mr. Virgil," and went walking the other way.

Down one street and up another he went to keep himself too from the sight of the boys playing. It was nothing to him today that he could not be out on the square with them, but he must keep apart to remember the better the memories in his head. He turned down the lane to his own house and opened the door of it. There was the stove waiting, choked with ash, to be cleaned and lighted. There were the vegetables, stiff as dead men on the table, waiting for water and fire to bring them life again.

The house was bleak and silent, but behind each door some menace seemed to linger. He thought of the father's voice singing, and of the mother's hand lifted to wipe the tears from her face. Even the goats up there were warm and soft with promise, and the strong male goats had turned gentle beside their children. He was thinking of these things and emptying the ashes from the stove, when somebody struck the window glass.

Chiesa was looking in from the street, and Young Palavicini crossed the kitchen and opened the window.

"Hello," said Chiesa.

"Hello," Young Palavicini said.

"What are you having for supper?" said Chiesa, and he drew his grin up sharp in his face. "We're having tomato sauce on our spaghetti!"

Young Palavicini saw the small black eyes button and unbutton uneasily before him.

"I know," said Chiesa, in scorn, "I know where you've been."

Young Palavicini lifted his hand to close the window, and Chiesa dropped his head as though expecting a blow. Then he began to titter aloud from the street where he stood.

"You've been with the outlaws," he said, hiding his mouth in his hand and his laughter. "You've been up to the monastery where the police are going to get them for cutting the trees down. My father passed there yesterday and he's going to tell what they done."

No thought had come or gone in Young Palavicini's head, but he turned and walked out of the kitchen and into his father's room. He walked to the table by the bed, and each move he made seemed shaped by preparation. This he had thought, or had dreamed, or had done in this same way before. He took the blue box from the drawer and took the cover from it, and then he climbed on the rush-bottomed chair, heedless of the muck on his boots, and took down his father's gun from the wall. Once it was loaded he went back to the kitchen and stood before the open window. Across the lane, Chiesa had his foot on his own doorstep and when Young Palavicini called out his name he spun around smiling.

ASTRONOMER'S WIFE

There is an evil moment on awakening when all things seem to pause. But for women, they only falter and may be set in action by a single move: a lifted hand and the pendulum will swing, or the voice raised and through every room the pulse takes up its beating. The astronomer's wife felt the interval gaping and at once filled it to the brim. She fetched up her gentle voice and sent it warily down the stairs for coffee, swung her feet out upon the oval mat, and hailed the morning with her bare arms' quivering flesh drawn taut in rhythmic exercise: left, left, left my wife and fourteen children, right, right, right in the middle of the dusty road.

The day would proceed from this, beat by beat, without reflection, like every other day. The astronomer was still asleep, or feigning it, and she, once out of bed, had come into her own possession. Although scarcely ever out of sight of the impenetrable silence of his brow, she would be absent from him all the day in being clean, busy, kind. He was a man of other things, a dreamer. At times he lay still for hours, at others he sat upon the roof behind his telescope, or wandered down the pathway to the road and out across the mountains. This day, like any other, would go on from the removal of the spot left there from dinner on the astronomer's vest to the severe thrashing of the mayonnaise for lunch. That man might be each time the new arching wave, and woman the undertow that sucked him back, were things she had been told by his silence were so.

In spite of the earliness of the hour, the girl had heard her mistress's voice and was coming up the stairs. At the threshold of the bedroom she paused, and said: "Madame, the plumber is here."

The astronomer's wife put on her white and scarlet smock very quickly and buttoned it at the neck. Then she stepped carefully around the motionless spread of water in the hall.

"Tell him to come right up," she said. She laid her hands on the banisters and stood looking down the wooden stairway. "Ah, I am Mrs. Ames," she said softly as she saw him mounting. "I am Mrs. Ames," she said softly, softly down the flight of stairs. "I am Mrs. Ames," spoken soft as a willow weeping. "The professor is still sleeping. Just step this way."

The plumber himself looked up and saw Mrs. Ames with her voice hushed, speaking to him. She was a youngish woman, but this she had forgotten. The mystery and silence of her husband's mind lay like a chiding finger on her lips. Her eyes were gray, for the light had been extinguished in them. The strange dim halo of her yellow hair was still uncombed and sideways on her head.

For all of his heavy boots, the plumber quieted the sound of his feet, and together they went down the hall, picking their way around the still lake of water that spread as far as the landing and lay docile there. The plumber was a tough, hardy man; but he took off his hat when he spoke to her and looked her fully, almost insolently in the eye.

"Does it come from the wash-basin," he said, "or from the other . . . ?"

"Oh, from the other," said Mrs. Ames without hesitation. In this place the villas were scattered out few and primitive, and although beauty lay without there was no reflection of her face within. Here all was awkward and unfit; a sense of wrestling with uncouth forces gave everything an austere countenance. Even the plumber, dealing as does a woman with matters under hand, was grave and stately. The mountains round about seemed to have cast them into the shadow of great dignity.

Mrs. Ames began speaking of their arrival that summer in the little villa, mourning each event as it followed on the other.

"Then, just before going to bed last night," she said, "I noticed something was unusual."

The plumber cast down a folded square of sackcloth on the brimming floor and laid his leather apron on it. Then he stepped boldly onto the heart of the island it shaped and looked long into the overflowing bowl.

"The water should be stopped from the meter in the garden," he said at last.

"Oh, I did that," said Mrs. Ames, "the very first thing last night. I turned it off at once, in my nightgown, as soon as I saw what was happening. But all this had already run in."

The plumber looked for a moment at her red kid

slippers. She was standing just at the edge of the clear, pure-seeming tide.

"It's no doubt the soil lines," he said severely. "It may be that something has stopped them, but my opinion is that the water seals aren't working. That's the trouble often enough in such cases. If you had a valve you wouldn't be caught like this."

Mrs. Ames did not know how to meet this rebuke. She stood, swaying a little, looking into the plumber's blue relentless eye.

"I'm sorry—I'm sorry that my husband," she said, "is still—resting and cannot go into this with you. I'm sure it must be very interesting. . . ."

"You'll probably have to have the traps sealed," said the plumber grimly, and at the sound of this Mrs. Ames' hand flew in dismay to the side of her face. The plumber made no move, but the set of his mouth as he looked at her seemed to soften. "Anyway, I'll have a look from the garden end," he said.

"Oh, do," said the astronomer's wife in relief. Here was a man who spoke of action and object as simply as women did! But however hushed her voice had been, it carried clearly to Professor Ames who lay, dreaming and solitary, upon his bed. He heard their footsteps come down the hall, pause, and skip across the pool of overflow.

"Katherine!" said the astronomer in a ringing tone. "There's a problem worthy of your mettle!"

Mrs. Ames did not turn her head, but led the plumber swiftly down the stairs. When the sun in the garden struck her face, he saw there was a wave of color in it, but this may have been anything but shame.

"You see how it is," said the plumber, as if leading her

mind away. "The drains run from these houses right down the hill, big enough for a man to stand upright in them, and clean as a whistle too." There they stood in the garden with the vegetation flowering in disorder all about. The plumber looked at the astronomer's wife. "They come out at the torrent on the other side of the forest beyond there," he said.

But the words the astronomer had spoken still sounded in her in despair. The mind of man, she knew, made steep and sprightly flights, pursued illusion, took foothold in the nameless things that cannot pass between the thumb and finger. But whenever the astronomer gave voice to the thoughts that soared within him, she returned in gratitude to the long expanses of his silence. Desert-like they stretched behind and before the articulation of his scorn.

Life, life is an open sea, she sought to explain it in sorrow, and to survive women cling to the floating débris on the tide. But the plumber had suddenly fallen upon his knees in the grass and had crooked his fingers through the ring of the drains' trap door. When she looked down she saw that he was looking up into her face, and she saw too that his hair was as light as gold.

"Perhaps Mr. Ames," he said rather bitterly, "would like to come down with me and have a look around?"

"Down?" said Mrs. Ames in wonder.

"Into the drains," said the plumber brutally. "They're a study for a man who likes to know what's what."

"Oh, Mr. Ames," said Mrs. Ames in confusion. "He's still—still in bed, you see."

The plumber lifted his strong, weathered face and looked curiously at her. Surely it seemed to him strange for a man to linger in bed, with the sun pouring yellow as

wine all over the place. The astronomer's wife saw his lean
cheeks, his high, rugged bones, and the deep seams in his
brow. His flesh was as firm and clean as wood, stained
richly tan with the climate's rigor. His fingers were blunt,
but comprehensible to her, gripped in the ring and holding the iron door wide. The backs of his hands were bound
round and round with ripe blue veins of blood.

"At any rate," said the astronomer's wife, and the
thought of it moved her lips to smile a little, "Mr. Ames
would never go down there alive. He likes going up," she
said. And she, in her turn, pointed, but impudently,
towards the heavens. "On the roof. Or on the mountains.
He's been up on the tops of them many times."

"It's a matter of habit," said the plumber, and suddenly
he went down the trap. Mrs. Ames saw a bright little piece
of his hair still shining, like a star, long after the rest of
him had gone. Out of the depths, his voice, hollow and
dark with foreboding, returned to her. "I think something
has stopped the elbow," was what he said.

This was speech that touched her flesh and bone and
made her wonder. When her husband spoke of height,
having no sense of it, she could not picture it nor hear.
Depth or magic passed her by unless a name were given.
But madness in a daily shape, as elbow stopped, she saw
clearly and well. She sat down on the grasses, bewildered
that it should be a man who had spoken to her so.

She saw the weeds springing up, and she did not move
to tear them up from life. She sat powerless, her senses
veiled, with no action taking shape beneath her hands. In
this way some men sat for hours on end, she knew,
tracking a single thought back to its origin. The mind of
man could balance and divide, weed out, destroy. She sat

on the full, burdened grasses, seeking to think, and dimly waiting for the plumber to return.

Whereas her husband had always gone up, as the dead go, she knew now that there were others who went down, like the corporeal being of the dead. That men were then divided into two bodies now seemed clear to Mrs. Ames. This knowledge stunned her with its simplicity and took the uneasy motion from her limbs. She could not stir, but sat facing the mountains' rocky flanks, and harking in silence to lucidity. Her husband was the mind, this other man the meat, of all mankind.

After a little, the plumber emerged from the earth: first the light top of his head, then the burnt brow, and then the blue eyes fringed with whitest lash. He braced his thick hands flat on the pavings of the garden path and swung himself completely from the pit.

"It's the soil lines," he said pleasantly. "The gases," he said as he looked down upon her lifted face, "are backing up the drains."

"What in the world are we going to do?" said the astronomer's wife softly. There was a young and strange delight in putting questions to which true answers would be given. Everything the astronomer had ever said to her was a continuous query to which there could be no response.

"Ah, come, now," said the plumber, looking down and smiling. "There's a remedy for every ill, you know. Sometimes it may be that," he said as if speaking to a child, "or sometimes the other thing. But there's always a help for everything amiss."

Things come out of herbs and make you young again, he might have been saying to her; or the first good rain will quench any drought; or time of itself will put a broken bone together.

"I'm going to follow the ground pipe out right to the torrent," the plumber was saying. "The trouble's between here and there and I'll find it on the way. There's nothing at all that can't be done over for the caring," he was saying, and his eyes were fastened on her face in insolence, or gentleness, or love.

The astronomer's wife stood up, fixed a pin in her hair, and turned around towards the kitchen. Even while she was calling the servant's name, the plumber began speaking again.

"I once had a cow that lost her cud," the plumber was saying. The girl came out on the kitchen step and Mrs. Ames stood smiling at her in the sun.

"The trouble is very serious, very serious," she said across the garden. "When Mr. Ames gets up, please tell him I've gone down."

She pointed briefly to the open door in the pathway, and the plumber hoisted his kit on his arm and put out his hand to help her down.

"But I made her another in no time," he was saying, "out of flowers and things and whatnot."

"Oh," said the astronomer's wife in wonder as she stepped into the heart of the earth. She took his arm, knowing that what he said was true.

I CAN'T GET DRUNK

Denka was a fine figure of an ostrich plume. I could do very well with you said I when first I saw him. He was drooping and molting across the bar. I'd curl you up on the irons, my lad, and pin you across the front of my hat. You'd look fine going into the casino at Monte Carlo riding a Leghorn brim. Oh would I said Denka. I don't know what's the matter with me. I can't get drunk.

It's my stomach said Denka. I could see it slightly swollen beneath his coat. He had no one to put back his buttons on his clothes when time had seized them by the forelock. To see him with his lean mouth closed like a wallet, his eye like iron and as cold as, would it ever have come into your head that the mouth of his heart was open, was gaping wide like a frog's in dry weather, requesting that into it be drained not glasses with frost on their faces but something else again. It was easy enough to see that his bottom was at ease nowhere except upon a stool at a bar but other things, if you had a mind to, you might see as well.

If you could forget yourself for two minutes you might see his eye peeled for the sight of a new face coming in, his ear harking for a word that would set him to thinking at last. Whatever you said to him it was drawn with labor word by word from the bog of his interest in something else. Up and down and around was he looking for something that might catch his curiosity. If I stay up all night was he thinking perhaps something will happen after all. By staying awake all night I might get a whiff of it. But what if it came to pass in the morning then, in the morning early when I was recovering from what my thirst had left me. It is not unthinkable, was his silence bespeaking as his head sought wearily this way and that with his glass lifted, that something might happen in the morning early and then where would I be?

If I learned a new language entirely I said to Denka would you listen to what I am trying to say to you?

I don't know said Denka I don't feel very well.

At this moment I myself gave up words. I let the conversation slip out the door and die like a windless flag on the lamppost. Maybe you could do something else for your heartache I was thinking except putting it to sleep. There he was rocking it back and forth at the bar like a cradle, humming a tune to it with a look on his face sour enough to have kept his sorrow awake with the vapors. There he was crying his anguish aloud and dancing with it. Down the barroom floor with a black-mammy tune fit to send pickaninnies scampering to papa for comfort. Lassoing slumber he was with the sides of his heels kicking. I'll sing that misery, warble that grief, I'll shout that sorrow into the middle of next year, so help me. Denka stopped dancing and sat down on the stool beside me. His cheeks were as white as paper.

I don't know what's the matter with me he said. I can't get drunk.

Denka came back from where he had been and he said There's something going on across the street. The record of it could be read in the faces of the people walking arm in arm back and forth among the tables. A night as hot as a warming pan of coals between your sheets. There's something going on said Denka. He looked for it in every eye that passed him by. A couple of words that slapped his ear he took and used them as his own. There's something going on he said. Where he couldn't remember. There's something happening around the corner. His ears were starting from his head to capture the direction of it. There's something happening somewhere else he said. Into these places and out of them we went. There's something happening on the other side of town said Denka. We stepped into a taxi to track it down. Before the café mirror we sat still and surveyed the landslide of our faces down the glass.

Your appearance is such a deceptive one I said.

What about your own said Denka with that paint all over your face.

Well what about it I said. You don't look like a man who could stand the weather. The trouble with you is I said that when the lightning struck you it hit you hard, it hit the bark right off you, it ripped you wide open with a scar down the side of you.

I'm getting along all right said Denka. His hands were traveling back and forth from bar to glass like nervous gentlemen, from hair to chin, settling their cuff links, eyeing the ladies entering or their escorts. Gauntlets of sunburn and harnesses of sweat were on them all as they walked in and sat their bottoms down. The trouble with me is said Denka I can't get drunk.

Once I got drunk said Denka. He began to laugh at the thought of it. He held on to the bar to keep from laughing. That day we went to La Turbie to buy a house. He stood holding on tight to his dry relentless laughter at the bar.

We had a long way to walk in the sun I said to him.

And I held up my hat over your head all the way said Denka as he swayed with laughter. I didn't know you so well then.

Who ever would see you now as a tree of shade and shelter I said to him. Can you picture yourself now spreading your boughs to keep the elements away?

Denka put down his head on the bar and laughed so hard that the tears ran out of his eyes.

What time of year was it anyway he said. I know I was hungry said Denka.

We had a fine lunch at Monte Carlo I said to him.

Yes said he but it wasn't enough. If you remember there were places for rabbits next to the stables.

You were going to buy blue rabbits and sell their hides for a living I said to him.

I must have been crazy said Denka. He leaned against the bar and his mouth was pulled across his face with laughing. I went around eating all the lilacs off the bushes I was so hungry. There was something else I was going to do.

You were going to restore the vineyards I said to him. They went down the hill step by step like ruins to the sea. Blight or greed had left them for fifty years without anyone so much as turning an eye on them. You were going to do something about the landscape. You were going to resurrect the land.

I must have been drunk said Denka.

Well what did you do then but insist upon drinking the Mediterranean. You climbed very prettily up on the granite and from where you sat you could take at least half of it out of sight in your hands. I'll put that under my belt you said with all its octopuses and corals. You can do what you like with your half said I but the other half is mine.

And what did I say to that said Denka.

You said I could waggle my tail to my heart's content in the brine of my half as long as I brought back my gills and fins in time for tea.

I must have been mad said Denka.

And didn't we set in that afternoon itself to cultivate the garden. Down on our knees we got and started to clear the weeds out from under the pines where they had no business to be. Out, out upon you leaf and root you said to the upstarts. The sleek brown Kelley-slide of needles was what you liked under your behind.

I did, did I said Denka. I was drunk as a lord that day.

And another time I got drunk said Denka. He threw back his head and began to yipe with laughter. The day we went to Corsica. He put his hand over his eyes and stood shaking with laughter at the bar.

We couldn't lie still for the moonlight I said it wouldn't let you sleep.

Nor would it said Denka.

We sat up all night with it, holding its hand and saying kind things to it. We rolled it up in a rug and told it stories in its ear.

What kind of things did we tell it said Denka. Would you like another drink?

Yes said I we told it a story about a little boy who had no mother and no father.

I must have been pretty tight said Denka.

So what did he do said I but run away from wherever he was without so much as a by-your-leave and go to work on a ranch in the West part of America.

I must have been soused said Denka.

And didn't he buy a gramophone before you could say how-do-ye-do and there he'd sit out on the prairie at night playing his gramophone records, nothing like you nor I would buy mind you, but Chinese songsters to cry down the sentiment, and Java drummers to beat out the wishies. He'd lie there at night so you said with his ear to the ground listening, harking all night for the sound of horses' riding or a grasshopper turning over in his grave.

And then what happened said Denka.

The moon up and waned on us said I and there we were sitting on the lowdown deck of the boat to Corsica holding hands over from the ladies' section to the men's.

I must have been crazy said Denka.

There were we sitting said I and what did you do but reach yourself over from the gentlemen's to the ladies' and kiss me good morning.

I must have been drunk said Denka sitting up all night that way.

Listen said he. There's something wrong with my stomach. Behind him had the dawn sprung up without warning, it was growing up straight as a hollyhock from out the fresh manure in the street.

I can't get drunk was what he said to me. He drank down his glass.

If you're around tonight he said we might have another try at it. We'll start right off mixing our drinks he said. His stool had rolled over and he could not place his hand upon it on the floor. We've been fools said Denka to keep stone sober on gin this way.

LETTERS OF A LADY

June 22, 1929

Sir Basil Wynns, M.D.
   Buxton, Cheshire
DEAR SIR,

Your name has been mentioned to me by one who has never ceased regretting your professional neglect; a neglect which, because it involved no *contretemps,* seems to be distinguished by an ethical integrity much too rarely evidenced in a decade of facile visits. The explanation of your reluctance and your ultimate refusal to continue visiting my friend has been given me in what I believe were your own words: that Cherokee women riding bareback, leaped from their horses and after giving birth, remounted and rode on again. Moved by a profound respect I now address you with the request that you call upon me in the interests of my daughter's health.

Yours faithfully,
SIBYL CASTANO

June 28, 1929

DEAR SIR,

As you have apparently not perceived of your loss, I am writing to call your attention to the fact that during your

visit to my home last week you left your medicine case in
the greenhouse. I had not visited the magentas again since
the afternoon you were so good as to appraise them, but as
I tended them this morning, pinching off as you suggested
those small leaves which uncurl wherever the stem is
joined to the stalk, I came upon your alligator case, so
mottled with sunlight that for a moment it gave me quite a
start, crouched as it was behind the muscat vines with the
elegance of an actual beast. Whatever your wish may be
concerning its disposition I shall be pleased to know.

Yours faithfully,
SIBYL CASTANO

June 30, 1929

DEAR SIR BASIL,

Upon my return from London last evening my servant
informed me that you had been here during the afternoon,
and I subsequently discovered your letter which, I pre-
sume, you neglected to hand him, and which you had let
fall among the magenta plants. I am grateful for the
information therein contained, and acting upon your
advice I set out this morning with my gardener the day-
lilies and the iris-root. They now form a triangle near the
hotbeds, one which I am sure would interest you as alien
to English design. This pleases me, for my admiration for
the precision of England has definite bounds. Because of
these very bounds my mind has begun to divide itself
concerning the schooling of my little girl. At teatime I am
persuaded by the sanctity of ease that all men should be
Englishmen and all women born in Spain. In other words,
that men should be taught to believe in the dignity of their

profession, to follow a life led by interminable niceties of the mind; and that women should be schooled to elaborate this masculine faith with an embroidery of fidelity and passion.

You said the other day that Juno should be educated as if she were a boy, but what, it has occurred to me, would then become of that single and personal thing which no education should touch, were she to be narrowed down to the perfected code of insular morality which for me signifies an English education? She would be permitted no curiosity, and no imagination, and while this might make her a better object for filial and domestic experiences, I for my part am not interested in her responsibility to me, but rather in her capacities for discriminate living. At teatime, however, I am reasonable, and I can therefore in reply to your request but recommend that moment of the day to you as decidedly my most satisfactory time for your next visit.

Yours sincerely,
SIBYL CASTANO

July 8, 1929

DEAR SIR BASIL,

I cannot tell you with what a degree of pleasure I received the blossoms from the hands of your gardener this morning! Let me relate the circumstances, which should make evident in some measure the greatness of my surprise and delight.

It was quite early in the day, and to recover from the confinement necessitated by putting jelly into glasses (a clear variety of lemon with slips of the rind set in it like crescent moons), I was on my knees at the flag-bed in the act of loosening the earth about those peculiarly native roots whose tenacity you know so well. Bowed as I was over the beds the raindrops which still lingered seemed to me as big as hawthorne flowers, and the marks of my little girl's sandals were filled with the enormous lace of spiderwebs which she had destroyed as she walked. Living as I do in absolute solitude I have time to observe such things as this, and frequently the pulp of a rug, the threads in a bit of homespun, and the pores of an orange skin, feather for hours the wings of my vision. So it was that at a moment when two roadways which the ants had worn between the umbrella trees were as clearly defined as the bed of a river and quite as broad to me, the boots of your gardener took root beside me.

I was so absorbed in the manipulation of ant eggs from black ant-hand to hand, and so unprepared for intrusion, that the basket of your flowers set suddenly down upon the grass caused me to cry out with pleasure. Your species of hypatica is as beautiful as it was unknown to me, and I have spent the past hour going over my plates of the genera-plants in an endeavor to place it. The splayed leaf genus I knew in Spain, for fully a quarter of the wine-garden was banked with it, but your variety is extraordinarily unlike a flower, more as if the foot of a bird had imprinted its delicate mark upon a leaf of wax. It brought to my mind a number of like similes which collectors of the minute have left outside the pattern of their appreciation, such as the inner structure of a walnut shell.

The miniature which you had already spoken of to Juno she herself discovered in the twist of raffia, and she has in great delight put it about her neck on a bit of velvet. I am sure it is a perfect one of its kind, but miniatures are to me so obvious in intent that they demand rather than repay admiration.

There is a glass of Barcelona jelly awaiting your approval at tea, but my thanks I could not keep so long and I hasten to send them to you.

Yours very sincerely,
SIBYL CASTANO

July 30, 1929

MY DEAR, DEAR FRIEND:

I know that you will be glad to learn that the timber has arrived for the garden house and the men ready to begin work under your direction.

My happiness during the past days in watching you laying out the plans for the grounds and making of sand and stone beauty as subtle as a wilderness, is sharp in my memory. Your constant presence here made me feel more and more how like a drifting ship is this estate without a master. Indeed, despite my faith in women's dauntlessness, I feel that I have mismanaged affairs, for I find myself again this month obliged to dispense with two more members of my gradually diminishing staff. This time I have asked Nora, whose fruitcake you once delighted me by praising, as well as one of the stableboys, to seek other employment. My cousin has kindly offered to advance me notes upon my securities, but I am loath to avail myself of assistance proffered by a gentleman to whom I can make no adequate return.

Forgive me for thus burdening you with my matters. One of your own great qualities is an ability to wholly efface your existence and its details from the minds of others, and when I consider how little or nothing I know of what your life may be comprised, I am shamed by my own volubility. You know so well *de facto* the solitary ways of my exile: that Juno is my entire life and that the word "Spain" in itself is for me as if one had opened a window upon a brilliant garden.

Very sincerely,
SIBYL CASTANO

Aug. 16, 1929

DEAR SIR BASIL,

In the four days which have elapsed since your visit, I have had ample time to reflect upon all that you had to say to me. In particular your remarks upon morality have lingered in my memory, for it has always seemed to me that a man never judges morality or the absence of it in a woman in any abstract way, but always in consideration of the degree to which the woman may attract him. Even more true is this of an Englishman, for while an Englishman is lost if he has not a tradition to direct his actions, it is true as well that the question of morality is so closely associated with flattery and with pleasure that even an Englishman discards tradition as absolutely worthless in this case and decides for himself.

If the woman herself does not offend his past, she has a sentimental claim upon him which is the equivalent of respect. A foreign woman I should think scarcely falls under this excerpta for an Englishman suspects all ways to knowledge but his own. It requires a certain insight at times to ignore a blindness as bewildering as an English-man's can be.

You spoke of marriage with such feeling to me that I am forced to believe it a greater concern of yours than you care to admit. Fidelity is to me the one quality that one can put one's fingers on, that one can possess to perfec-tion, and yet it remains a quality rarely perfectly con-ceived. Marriage as an ethical state for that quality seems to me as satisfactory as can be any law when narrowed to the point of a personal application. Hence your remarks upon the free nature of love I cannot take seriously as my life has been lived upon principles so antithetic to those you sponsor that I find them strange and flavorless.

But the discussion has interested me immeasurably, and in particular because it was discussed from the viewpoint of an Englishman, that is to say, a man whose first twenty years are entirely devoted to learning alternatives for avoiding that which he really wishes to say.

Juno asks me to send you all manners of salutations. I begin to find her already maturing, and her changing contours have this summer persuaded me more than ever how greatly do we both need the balance between us of an intelligence that has been directed and enriched by life itself and not merely by a contemplation of it.

Your sincere friend,
SIBYL CASTANO

Aug. 18, 1929

DEAR SIR BASIL,

It was indeed good of you to send me the photograph of your wife and two children.

As I look upon this cheerful evidence of your sane and
happy hearth, I cannot but think how triply blessed you
are by the sweet dependency of three such, shall I say,
human faces? While I am indeed flattered by the attention
you have thus shown me, I am somewhat at a loss to
determine the reasons motivating your generous gesture.
As you had not at any time mentioned your happy
connections to me it can hardly be that you send me the
photograph with the wish to share with one so casually
known to you as myself the indicated intimacy of your
family circle.

On the other hand I have too much regard for the
delicacy of your taste to imagine that this evidence has
been proffered me in explanation of your suggestions to
me concerning the freedom of affections despite the fetters
of the church.

I am therefore returning the photograph to you by
special messenger, and with my deepest gratitude to you
for permitting me this brief but enlightening glimpse into
your existence. In conclusion, I fear that our arrange-
ments for lunch for the day after tomorrow must now be
indefinitely postponed as I am called quite unexpectedly
to St. Sebastian to attend a number of family functions
pertinent to deaths and births.

Yours sincerely,
SIBYL CASTANO

Aug. 19, 1929

DEAR SIR BASIL,

I have received your telegram at the moment and I
hasten to assure you how fully I understand and sympa-

thize with you in your predicament. I can readily see how grievously your wife must take to heart the presumable loss of the miniature, which in reality you were good enough to present to my daughter. But consider as well the depths of Juno's sorrow were I to exact from her its return. I regret indeed the unfortunate circumstances, but I cannot see my way clear to demanding an immature understanding of an adult's indecisions. I must therefore ask you, as well as your little family, to content yourself with the grass basket and the twist of raffia, which, with the dahlia bulbs, my servant is returning to your greenhouse this afternoon.

Yours sincerely,
SIBYL CASTANO

ART COLONY

Paris has a grief of its own on some nights in December. If you walked the streets all night with it, you could not make it sleep. A drenching blast of snow worn thin swings down the steps of the Métro. It combs your hair out long on your face, and dries its tears with your hands.

Such a piece of its violence blew in through the door with the young woman. She came in from the street and turned the lock, and stood breathing deep and looking awhile before her. There was a yellow bulb left burning beyond in the kitchen, as good as a lemon squeezed out and the sallow drops of it falling. *Hush, hush*, said the wily step of the snow outside pacing the long bare windows of the room.

The house was cold, and down the length of the table stood the dishes and disorder left over from supper. The warmest things in the place were the mouse and her young scampering off from the rinds of cheese left there by the dozen people who had eaten. The shy little beasts went scattering and whistling away when Shiloh threw her cap down and walked across the room. Three woodcuts, as wide as posters, waved from the walls in the sharp draughts of air that came and went like the lifting of a fan: one of a man spading in a rich field, another of a muscular archer setting an arrow to his bow, and another of a strong man sowing handfuls of golden grain. The wooden seats that stood against the walls were covered with soiled, woolly hides.

The range stood black and burdened in the corner, piled up with the day's dishes and wigged with long, thick curls of shining grease. "Blessèd is the artisan," said the poster in block letters pinned above it on the plaster, "for his is the joy of creation." The sink was clogged with strips of salad and match butts, and Shiloh gathered up the small bouquet of refuse in her fingers. She turned on the water and, as the pan filled, she stared mindlessly ahead at the photograph that hung over the spigot. Whenever Shiloh turned on the water at night to heat it for the dishes, there stood the photograph before her of a strong, beautiful woman in a tunic, with her arms stretched out from the picture. Under her was printed: "I would teach the whole world to dance!"

Shiloh waited there at night in the cold with the stalk of fresh water falling between them, looking a long while at the face of the strong, dead woman. She had not known her alive, but the long, humorous upper lip and the shapely arms were like Sorrel's. She stood quiet, with her wet coat still buttoned over, and looked at the face of Sorrel's dead sister, and the water brimmed up to the edge of the pan and rippled over. I used to believe in it, she thought: in Sorrel, in the old Roman, an old man with great white ropes of hair, standing clean and tall, like his sister, on his bare sandaled feet.

I used to believe in it, she thought as she set a match to

the gas. Everything all about lay deep and foul in its own dirt. Whenever he spoke, I believed in the action of poetry, and in the door standing wide for anybody at all who might be wanting shelter. But if ever she said: "There are some nights in December or some other times when I can't come back to it," he would roll himself up in his toga and cry to himself for weeks.

She went upstairs, two at a time, but softly. The rooms above were dark, but from the light on the landing she could see there was a woman sitting still on the floor. She was sitting near to the bench where the child must be sleeping. Her head was bowed, as though in sleep, and a part ran up the middle. She had drawn the woven rug around her for warmth, for there were no fires to bring comfort to the night.

Shiloh stepped into the dark, chill room, silently around the woman. Strangers, disciples of Sorrel's, often came and went, but this one she had never seen before. She could see the child's face shining on the black, woolly hide that lay beneath its head, and stooped to touch the child's cheek with her fingers. Suddenly the woman near the open door raised up her fallen head and swung her face around.

"Who's there?" she said sharply. Shiloh could see her stiffen and rear against the light.

"What are *you* doing, sitting there?" said Shiloh indolently out of the darkness. She felt the child's hands bloodless as snow on the shaggy cover. In the dark she took off her coat and laid it over the shape that was sleeping there.

"I'm here all right," said the woman sharply. "I'm here, but I'll get out pretty God damn quick."

She spoke with an accent, but scarcely, and Shiloh could see against the light the fierce, wild angles of her face. Her evil neck reached out of her clothes, and her viperous tongue turned sharp on Shiloh. "What do you have to be touching that baby for?" she said. "It was me who got it to sleep, it wasn't you."

Shiloh sat down on the floor close to the bench and lit a cigarette in the darkness. She opened her mouth in the cold and breathed the warm smoke over the child's fingers in her palm. The stale weather in the room went icily up and down her spine, and the woman rolled up in the rug on the other side sat shaking.

"You ain't got no reason to come and set in waking it," said the woman. "None of you have no care for it," she said bitterly. "It didn't have no supper before I come along. All of you coming in at any hour it pleases you. They was all dressed up going out to the moving pictures when I come along."

"Where are you from?" said Shiloh out of the darkness. So many came and went on again that it was of no interest any more.

"I came up third from Marseilles," said the woman's sour voice. "I walked that way from the *gare* because I didn't have as much as the Métro fare."

"That's one way of getting warm," said Shiloh languidly. She felt the south wind of her own breath blowing on the child's white hands.

"You don't know nothing I been through with!" the woman shouted out in grief. She drew herself into the rug and sat dark and mourning by the door. "You come and go in your sheets and your shawls and live the way you please!"

"Why did you come here to Sorrel?" said Shiloh in a little while.

"Hell," said the woman, "I knew the old guy in Germany." She threw up her sharp, thin head in anger. The thought of something else had stirred her scalding bile. "To hell with him and his tribe," she said, "if they wasn't in hell already! This place is as like it as anything I ever seen. I tell you, I'm Russian and I beat it through the revolution, but I never hope to see worse than this place," she said.

Her hands came out like scrawny men against the light, and scratched their hollow spines aloud with her nails.

"That baby there!" she cried out suddenly in fury. "Why don't they put talcum powder on it like they do on other babies? That's what I asked them. Little thing not more than two years old. I come to the door and they had their glad rags on, dressed up like a lot of Arabs setting off to the moving pictures. Here's your part in the colony, says Sorrel, set where you are and look to the house. As if I was to wash up their filth after them. I ain't had no supper. I found the baby crying. It's got a bottom sore like a chimpanzee."

Shiloh sat smoking with the child's fingers against her mouth. A shadow of warmth was stealing now across its flesh.

"Young ones like you," said the Russian woman with venom, "got no ideas in your head but your own lookout! I've known a lot of your sort," she said, "all I want to know. To hell with the old ones, you say. You got no kick coming."

"What were you doing in Marseilles?" said Shiloh after a little.

"Hell," said the woman, "I got stranded."

They sat quiet in the dark, icy room, harking to the child's breath coming and going.

"I ain't used to anything like this," the woman said. "I was ten years with the Baroness von Hoffen," she said, and her bitter voice had turned to sorrow. "We been living all the time on Riverside Drive, and on the Champs Élysées, and on the Riviera. She's an American, always spending her money on Sorrel's bum rugs and scarves and things."

Her voice went small and grim in her throat as the thoughts came to her.

"She believes in the artists, eh! She ought to get a night sleeping on the floor! She fell for the artistic life and bought sandals and tunics off him and went around half-naked too. She ain't got no use for the Baron except his money. She shipped me," said the Russian woman in sorrow. "She give me the gate because she thought it was me had give her away. I don't know how she's making out without me," she said after a moment. "She can't do her own hair for a nickel, and it was always me made every stitch for her, copying after models."

"Did you ever know Sorrel's sister?" Shiloh said.

"Whenever we went to the grand hotels," said the Russian woman, "she used to come along. She cried in the Ritz in London at the table because they didn't have no silver plate for her to eat her asparagus from. There was nothing alike between the two," she said. "The sister was always at the brother. You ain't the only one to know them," the Russian woman said.

"I didn't know his sister," said Shiloh. She lit another cigarette and sat back with her legs stretched out in the dark.

"She taught the Baroness to dance," said the Russian woman with her voice turned proud. "They used to dance on the Dutch beaches, jumping up and down. But the

Baroness couldn't run so fast, and she'd get left behind her. Hell, the sister'd come into the room in Germany when Sorrel had the colony. Set down a bottle of whisky and a beefsteak thicker than your arm, and say hell, Sorrel, to hell with your vegetation! Give these poor guys a meal for a change! He'd stand there and cry, her brother, and then she'd start in crying with him and smoothing him down. But she'd have some one cook her the beefsteak just the same. A good thick one," said the Russian woman eagerly, "running with juice and cooked up with French frieds. I knew how she liked them. It was me that made them right for her sometimes. She loved hollandaise sauce like money, and she'd eat it with a spoon. She used to like to start off with artichokes," said the Russian woman, "and them big American olives—"

"Listen, *ma vieille,*" said Shiloh. "I'll go down and cook us something for supper. It's ten o'clock at night, but that's not such a bad hour."

The Russian woman looked suddenly toward Shiloh.

"Ain't you had nothing to eat neither?" she said.

Shiloh slipped her hand away, softly, slowly, from the embrace of the child's warm fingers.

"I cook something for myself every night after I get home," she said. She saw the Russian woman's head lifted curiously to watch her step across the room to the lighted door. In the kitchen the water was boiling on the gas.

In a little while the woman came down the stairs with the rug folded over her shoulders. She moved cautiously down, without sound, like a specter in the hall. She was yellow as saffron in the face and her thin hair hung from her starving skull. There was naught but a bone or two of her body left under the hanging clothes.

The woman followed her wherever she went, swaying, like a woman drunk with weariness and sorrow. She helped Shiloh stack the thick, foul dishes and bear them in to the sink.

"Sit down there and warm yourself at the gas," said Shiloh. Whatever she did, the Russian woman stood by looking curiously at her face. The pile of dishes slid down and settled in the soapy water, and Shiloh turned to break the eggs into the pan.

"What is it you have to do all day?" said the woman shyly in a moment.

"Oh, I sell Sorrel's things at the shop," said Shiloh. "That's what gets me home so late."

"Hell," said the Russian woman, "you got a pretty face. Ain't there nothing better you can do?"

Shiloh sliced the few remaining cold potatoes in and watched them browning sweetly in the butter. The other woman stood up from the chair, and her face hung, avid and thirsting, above the steaming pan.

"The Baroness," said the Russian woman softly, "she used to like nothing better than a roasted chicken. When Sorrel's sister would come in, they'd finish one between them in no time at all."

Shiloh slid the eggs off onto a plate, and they carried their supper in, side by side, to the big, bare room. All around in the bleakness could Sorrel's craft be seen: his woodcuts, his tapestries, his handmade rugs standing upright, like dead men, in the corners.

"My God," said the Russian woman, beginning to eat, "I'll get out of here in a hurry! The Baroness'll send me the fare. I know how she is. She kicked me out, but that ain't all there is to it. She thought it was me told the Baron

about her and Sorrel, but I never gave her away." They sat
close together in the cold room, with the food beginning to
warm their bodies. "In ten years," said the Russian
woman with sorrow, "I never gave them away."

They took the dry cheese apart between them and laid
the parings as well, flat on their bread, and chewed side by
side.

"When I joined," said Shiloh slowly as she ate, "we
were going to work the hand press." She looked around
the room at the disorder, and grinned at the Russian
woman. "We were going to print poetry, and revive the
dramy," she said. "But nothing ever came of it. Sorrel got
some money and bought a new car instead."

"What's keeping you from clearing out?" said the
Russian woman. Shiloh wiped her plate clean leisurely
with a crust of bread, and then she shrugged her shoulders.

"One thing and another," she said.

"My God," said the Russian woman, "I'll write to the
Baroness tomorrow. She won't get anyone to be like I was
with the children. Sorrel used to give her hell," she said
bitterly, "about mother-loving your own."

"Yes," said Shiloh. She felt the woman fixed small and
terrible in grief beside her.

After a little while the Russian woman said: "Don't the
mother of that baby upstairs ever come here and see it?"

"Yes," said Shiloh slowly, "she comes sometimes."

"Ain't she got no money or what?" said the Russian
woman.

"No," said Shiloh. She saw her own hand playing
slowly with the crumbs left on the table. "She hasn't any
money," said Shiloh, "and its father's dead."

WINTER IN ITALY

He did not keep us waiting at all, but he came straight into the room, a tall, elegant-looking man, with his dark eyes quick and gay. There was scarcely any flesh on his bones, his hair was black and came to a point on his forehead, and he was wearing his long white smock because he was a surgeon and ready for purity at any instant. He was still young, and he had a small, a very pretty smile that he gave at once to you. It might have belonged to somebody else, it was peculiar in the rest of his face, small and shaped like a bright heart. He had a special sort of beauty that danced black as fury in his bold, quick eyes.

His name was Dr. Contento and we had never seen him before. We came there with a card from Dr. Paparini saying who we were. After Dr. Paparini had felt behind my ear, he said: "I think you'd better run along to Dr. Contento." Mother jumped up so quickly that her bag slipped from her knees, and her lipstick and her gloves and her thin blue handkerchief fell out on the doctor's rug.

"Please tell me at once what it is," she said. "You must tell me, Dr. Paparini, exactly what Lorenzo has."

"I don't know," said Dr. Paparini. He was writing her name out on the card before him. "That's why you must go to Contento. He's our ear man here, you know."

Contento was very beautiful, and from the minute he came into the room where we were waiting, he never took his eyes from mother's face. He saw it was mother who was afraid of what might be coming, and while he touched my head with his thumbs, he said to her: "How do you like the climate here? Isn't it exceptional?" And mother said: "You must tell me at once, please, what could possibly be the matter. You must promise not to keep things from me. That's the only thing I can't bear."

She kept dropping her cigarette ashes over his rug and pulling her little veil down to the end of her nose. She looked at me sitting in the steel chair under the shining bulb, and suddenly she stopped moving, and she stood there, quiet, like a portrait of my mother, with the hair yellow, and the lashes long, and coral rouge on her mouth.

"He plays the piano so well," she said in an unhappy voice. "Last winter we were in Mallorca, swimming the entire season. We want to get off for Switzerland as quickly as we can, now, for the skiing. He has to go on with his languages and music. I'm sure nothing's really the matter." And then her voice broke, and she said: "Doctor, you must tell me! I *have* to know."

"I had the pleasure of hearing you sing 'Tosca' last night," said Dr. Contento. He was pressing the side of my head with his fingers and giving his eyes and his smile to mother as he talked.

I said: "You hurt me. It's been hurting a week like that."

"But he had to hear me sing last night," said mother,

not caring about the tears running down her face. "He insisted on going, and he had no fever, so I let him. He put cotton in his ear to go. But of course he took it out when the music started."

"My wife and I agreed ," said Dr. Contento, "that you were the most brilliant 'Tosca' ever heard here."

"It's my favorite rôle," said mother, wiping her tears a little.

"My wife admired your blue gloves,"said Dr. Contento.

"Chanel," said mother. She took out her powder puff and smoothed it over her nose.

"Do sit down,"said Dr. Contento. He swung around on his little stool and took the shining eye of light from his forehead. His back, in its white, starched blouse, was turned to me, and he was facing mother. "We're used to good voices here," he said, "but you have that, you see, and everything else besides. I told my wife at the time that to me you were a miracle, you were the divine Tosca—"

"I do hope your wife agreed with you," said mother, and she was smiling at him.

"My wife—" Dr. Contento began, and then he gave a shrug of his shoulders. "Well," he said, "to return to our boy here, there'll have to be a little operation. It's a clear case of mastoid," he said.

We went to the hospital in the morning, and the nuns put me into bed and turned me on one side and shaved the half of my head. Mother and I were playing checkers together when Dr. Contento came in wearing a topcoat and carrying his soft gray hat in his hand. He said to her:

"Come to the light so I can see if you've been crying."

"I haven't been crying," said mother, and she went with him to the window. "I know what it is now, and I can be

brave. Only they've shaved his head, half of it, do you see?
Like prison. Half of his head belongs to the state now, but
the other half is mine."

They stood in the light of the window, and Dr. Contento's quick, long fingers had dropped on mother's arm.

"It's going to be nothing," he said. "I've done three
this afternoon." He was looking down at her face, and he
touched the bunch of violets on her shoulder. "But you,"
he said. "Somebody ought to be looking after you while
this is going on."

He could not take his eyes from her, or his fingers from
her arm.

"Oh, me?" said mother in a low voice. "I don't matter.
I've got used to being without anyone long ago."

"There are a few things," said Dr. Contento, and his
eyes were black and brilliant in his face, "one shouldn't
have to get used to."

Suddenly he crossed the room and took his coat off and
threw it down across a chair. Then he came to the bed and
touched the shaved side of my head. But still he might
never have seen me, for he turned away at once and strode
back to the window where mother was standing.

"You know, you're pale as death," he said, and he lifted
her fingers up as if to breathe some life upon them. "It
would be good if you stayed a while in this climate. You
need it," he said, and when mother lifted her eyes and
looked at him, she swayed upon her feet. "It would be
good for the boy's health, for recuperating . . ." Dr.
Contento said quickly. He was so thin, standing watching
her face, that his belly seemed scooped away inside his
clothes.

"I don't know if we have time to stay on here," said

mother softly. What of the skiing, my heart said to her in silence, what of the good two months ahead of snow? But Dr. Contento had dropped her hand from his, and "Time!" he cried out in anger. "What do you know of anything like that? You've had time for singing—for being beautiful—for being a woman," he said and he flung the five fingers of his open hand in contempt at her violets and her tight black dress. "I've never had the time to do what I wanted, never," he said. "Look at me," he ordered her, and when she raised her eyes, his voice grew quiet. "I've never even had the time to be a man," he said.

"Perhaps—we might stay a little—a little while," said mother, and Dr. Paparini opened the door without knocking and walked into the room.

"Hello," he said, and he took my hand. Dr. Contento turned around from the window. He looked at the watch on his narrow wrist and then he said in a level voice: "You're just ten minutes late, Papi."

"There's a lot of flu keeping me busy," said Dr. Paparini with a smile. He was an old man, with no hair on his head, but Dr. Contento was the leader because he was as quick as light. He followed Contento into the operating room after me, and he watched the nuns tie my wrists and ankles down, and then the two of them fastened their white masks over their faces.

"It's just as I told you, Papi," said Dr. Contento as he lifted his rubber gloves from the basin of disinfectant, "your whole future is ruined if you stay where you are. You'll have to make a move. I tell you the house I telephoned you about is exactly the thing for you—good neighborhood, imposing appearance—"

Paparini laughed behind his mask.

"It's very good of you, Contento," he said. "And perhaps you could tell me too where I'm to get the things that are necessary to go with it? I mean," he said, waving one rubber-encased hand, "the gilt chairs, and the bronze statues of Mercury, and the ancestors in their frames—"

"Good God," said Dr. Contento. He was setting the instruments out on the glass tabletop beside me. "Those things are going cheap now! The flu you've got on hand now ought to cover that. And a couple of good foreign cases," said Dr. Contento, "ought to set you up in fine style."

The nun came in carrying the chloroform box wrapped in a towel and took her place behind me.

"Breathe in," said Dr. Contento shortly. "Look here, Papi," he said. "A mastoid a day takes care of me nicely. This is my fourth this afternoon, and this one done in sterling. What do you think of that?"

Dr. Paparini leaned his masked face over me. I could see his eyes above the white.

"It's going to be all right," he said softly. "It's going to be a gentle sleep for a little while."

"Breathe in, breathe in," said Dr. Contento. "God damn you, Sister, hold it where he can get it!"

The chloroform box closed, humming, upon my face.

THE MEETING OF THE STONES

. . . for they sacrificed newborn babes at the sowing-time, older children when the grain had sprouted, and when it was fully ripe they sacrificed old men. . . .

His daughter had been on the doorstep, waiting, and seen him fall to the curb when the blood had whacked the base of his reason from under: Coppelia, with her skirts short, a little girl then, thinking that father had taken a tumble and no more than that, and running fast to pick up his instruments that had scattered out all over the street: his drawing pen, and his compass, and his little glass eye-screw for seeing things as they were in relation to plane surfaces.

Father had been an architect, and even now the remains of it could be seen in the ends of his thumbs, flexible as a mason's trowel to slap into troughs of fresh mortar. His hands were fashioned for use: for contriving the habitations of men, and rapping out the sound heart of timber; but now they lay still on the cover laid over his halted flesh, the nails clean but with no moons rising in them, the dark veins bloated as though lashed fast to stone. At

forty he had been stricken; the blow from behind in his
blood had felled him like a tree, and for seven years had he
lain motionless with his eyes thrashing in his head; for
seven years his eyes careening in fear that the threat were
still behind him, ready to strike again, and he forever
unable to rise and get away.

The sun of the coast had been vaunted to them as a
balm to the flesh and soothing to him, but he had no
respect for it. He might have been anywhere else except in
this idle part where nothing flourished beyond carnations
for the perfume factories, and grapes for pressing. He
might have been walled in by other people's houses for all
he had any time for the sight of the bay outside the
windows. He wanted Coppelia's drawing board held up
before him, and talk from her mouth of what she intended
to get on with, for Coppelia was now the architect. His
hands lying mute on the cover had asked it for years of her.
It goaded her, it lashed her fine, it left her no time for
womanly occupations; she must be this other manly thing
to give him excuse for breathing in and out at all.

He could say no word, but in his blood there was
ceaseless strong movement weaving. He never moved
hand nor limb, but his eyes were bowled strong as wooden
balls down the alley of his vision, smashed through whatever toppled, and returned solid and bellowing as wood to
his daughter's gentle face. She knew she was beautiful
because they lingered on her, and she knew as well that
this was not enough. Here was his strong shaven mouth,
and her own hand tipping the spoons of morning coffee in,
and his eyes questioning her about which detail of the
work she would be at when they were done. His hair was
faded out as white as milk, showing the clean scalp under

it. Beautiful little spiders of blood had spun their webs all over his stony face. The mouth's bow was shapely, rocked this way and that by the various thoughts that passed through his head, as though through a land-locked sea. Father at twenty must have made the heart leap high. The nose had not lowered its crest, surely, and the eye was still a light shining blue. Blue as well was the bay beyond, a precarious clear blue that might at any moment shatter into bits. Already the white horns of it, she saw, were bolting in the wind.

They had been a fortnight at work on the drawing: a temple to shade a plot of grass and the stone benches in Mr. Dooley's garden, to spare him from the sun on his high property. He would come in on them from day to day to see how one stone was being designed to meet another: a man with a taste for soft loose clothes, and wearing long mustaches; neither old nor young, but idle and forbearing in his manner; that his family had supplied the Empire with whisky for fifty years was something he took no trouble to speak of. But whenever he came into the room, the breath ran thin in Coppelia's mouth, and if she were sitting she must stand up, and if she were standing she must sit down again.

"Ah, Satan's Seat!" said Mr. Dooley, chiding with his cane the white wolfhound's curiosity for the room. "Oh, I think you're doing it beautifully, with such comprehension! Such a gift, such a gift," he said and turned to Coppelia's father sitting immune as a statue in his chair. Pleasure fled into Coppelia's face, and she lifted her hand to her lips as though to quell the delight that was rising there. Her father's halted flesh had walled her in forever, and this man the first with the ease and grace to scale it.

"Father directs every line of it," said Coppelia, avoiding Mr. Dooley's flagrant eyes.

"Yes, ah, yes," said Mr. Dooley, "yes," but he was giving her the compliment of believing this never to be true. He shook himself in his soft gray jacket and turned to the drawing stretched out on the board. "Now what would those little round pots there be, please?" he said. "Ah, the bases! The bases of the columns! Not the baseball bases? Ha, ha," laughed Mr. Dooley. "You never can tell, you know, what an American might be tempted to do! Ah, this is the ground plan, ah, I see, I see!" He put the head of his cane, the small silver skull, into his mouth and eyed the drawing. "For a moment I took them for little *pots de chambre,*" he said, and he wiped the skull clean in the palm of his hand. "Silly of me, what?"

Though Coppelia did not turn her head she sensed the wild roar of blood through her father's flesh; she knew his eyes leapt at the reins of blood that bound them, took the bit in their teeth, and raced up the studio walls.

"And of course I think the figures you've sketched in here lovely, really lovely," said Mr. Dooley, smoothing the laughter from his piquant face. "But what do you think? Do you think it might be nice with a male figure or two interspersed, as it were, amongst these others—? Perhaps a boy here, and another standing there, you know, in the general scheme," and his delicate hand shaped in suggestion over the board.

Coppelia stood staring, close to his side where he himself had come, her eyes fixed on the sketch laid out on tracing paper.

"But," said Coppelia, scarcely uttering, scarcely heard. "But you see it's the Maiden's Well, Mr. Dooley. This frieze," she said with her pencil out, "this shows the damsels come to draw water in bronze pitchers for their father's house. Isn't it, father?" She turned to look over her shoulder, turning in appeal to him, but there sat father in iron fury with his eyes swinging in his head.

"Yes, I see," said Mr. Dooley in doubt. "I see, of course." He gave a gentle sigh and looked back at the drawing again. "I just thought you might be able to work a Greek boy in here and there," he said. Then he smiled suddenly at Coppelia. "But I don't want to seem difficult in the least." He pulled one chamois glove on, and he said: "You yourself, you're so Greek, you know, so Grecian. Slim as a vase," said Mr. Dooley, looking upon her as though upon a work of art. "With that splendid boyish head set on your neck and shoulders. A sculptor would go mad at the sight of you," he said, and then he turned, speaking now to father. "Don't you see what I mean?" he said. He spoke so innocently and unaware, for the charging of father's eyes could mean nothing to him, and he read no anger in father's static flesh. "Ah, we'll have another talk about it," he said, "about the figures. I think it rather fitting, you know, if it is really Satan's Seat, that a male disciple or two be in attendance."

With this he left them, and Coppelia crossed the room to watch him from the window. The smell of his coat, and the cigarette he smoked were lingering still on the air. She pressed her brow against the pane, and her senses were turned as soft as satin. In a moment the door below would open and he would walk out on the road. She could not stir and relinquish this, although she knew of the violent pacing of father's eyes behind her. She felt her heart gone hard and cruel with ardor, laid over with an impervious

veneer of wild desire. Had her father been perishing, she
could not now have turned and flung out her hands to save
him. In another minute Mr. Dooley came out the door.

She sat down at the drawing board, and there was the
Englishman's face before her. She dared not touch her
pencil but sat fumbling the art gum up and down the
board's wood where fingers of dirt seemed to be. Under
her rubbing the timber shone forth fresh and white, and
the art gum rolled away in little crumbs of blackness. In a
while she found her hand was empty and the great square
of gum lay all about in wisps on the studio floor. She did
not turn her head, but she spoke, as if casually, to her
father: "I'm cleaning the drawing off," she said.

In a moment she would begin to work; in just a moment.
But the Englishman was in every corner of her mind. She
knew that if ever he spoke out to her that she would have to
do whatever he asked of her; shaking or crying or rejoicing,
she would have to go with him, for that was the way things
had to be. She had never dwelt on herself as separate from
her father's flesh, but now: someday I may get married, she
thought, and father will have to accustom himself to it.
When the grain was fully ripe, she thought, then it was the
time for the old men to go.

The grass withered white as early as June in this part of
the country, so a fountain must play from under the
temple to refresh the sod. And so had father's inflexible
will enjoined: the edifice must be broad and bold in aspect
to match the bold broad foliage of the south. In a fancy
land should stand at least one emblem of simplicity:
Demeter and Persephone wrenched from the stone fists of
this sterile ground. Here would Demeter sit, with her face
shrouded, grieving in the shadow of the olive tree beside

the Maiden's Well. To the north side would stand Persephone, her arms laid with the stalks of long flowers, and
the pomegranate seed resting on her broad lifted hand.
The majestic bones of these two fair women held the
temple's lintel on high. As in Greek times, the sculpture
would symbolize the purpose of the building: in this case a
portion of shade provided, like fertility, bringing relief to a
barren blistered land. On the south cornice, facing the
sea, would be graven: "The corn will not sprout until
Persephone is restored to me," and Persephone, standing
towards the north and looking to the heart of France
where, far from sight, the brimming Loire watered fresh
fertile land, would bear the inscription: "The expanse of
the plain will be transformed into a vast sheet of ruddy
corn."

Father had fallen asleep in his chair, and she worked the
day in silence; she was as solitary as if he had died and left
her alone. Was her gift so slight, she thought, that it could
not flourish without him? Could no other man pick and
revile the weaknesses that always missed her eye? She had
been a long time sacrificed to him and his taste, and now
some portion of himself must be severed and cast away. He
had given no sign of his impatience with Mr. Dooley, but
father's eyes might blaspheme and damn, for once she
would defy him. If he spat out his anger from his eye, the
shellac on her heart would settle fast; however he took it,
she would draw the Greek boys in.

In the evening, when his eyes had started open, she set
up the board before father. She waited, quivering but
stern, by his side, to see what his judgment would be.
However the storm broke, she knew it would not shake
her; she was rooted stern and firm in a new springing soil.

But in a minute he closed his lids down, and his sorrow came flooding out from under; his grief ran quickly down the stony slopes of his face, endlessly, as though it would never be spent. When she saw that he was weeping, she did not falter, but spoke to him in her hard new voice. "Father, do not cry."

She said "do not cry, father," but she had never looked for this warm melting flood. It washed down clear from his eyes and laved his long bleached jowls. Coppelia's tongue was dry with pain, but there were the heads of the Greek boys, irrevocable, lovely as women in the frieze, the orbs of their young eyes swollen blind in sandstone, and their hair crimped tight on their heroic brows. They stood intermingling their bare slender limbs with the long tunics of the maidens, and because of their beauty she would not slake her throat at the flowing stream of her father's grief. Cold and quaking, she stood relentless by his side.

"I don't know why you take it so," she said bitterly. "The first time, the first time I ever—. It's not just one person's preference over another's." She was thinking of the Englishman with every word she spoke. "It's quite appropriate," she said. "Of course there must have been young men sometimes at the well—Pluto's followers, perhaps—young men come to get a glimpse of the king's daughters, even—"

But his eyes suddenly flashed wide, knocked in the sockets, and shouted his impatience. He was closed dumb in his motionless body, held tight forever, stifling for speech with his tongue swollen thick with silence. His eyes struck at the granite of his flesh: out, out, let me out to fling my weapons! And Coppelia stood sly and faithless before their fury. She saw him a righteous man, a man of virtue; a monster who had never been corrupted nor won. He was fixed in virtue, in the mold of its unforgiving shape; if the use of his limbs were still his, Coppelia knew he would have struck her in the face.

But the next day came in fair and listless as these southern mornings came. It might well be the last, she thought, or near it, for now with this wedge driven between them the season seemed to be altering as well. Under her hand rolled the tides of light gray washes, basked and dried, and the paper tightened on the board. An endless wonder how the deep undulations were sucked shallow and smooth once the wash was dry. A wonder forever how the sun through the window made a screen of yellow light about the shadow she sat in. The open panels of it were warm as a fire burning in the room. It might well be the last drawing, she thought, for who could say how life might alter. Up swept the pale green turf to the steps of the temple and halted. In the afternoon she would put the clouds and the foliage in.

With each full dark drenching tear from the brush, she thought of Mr. Dooley. The names of many cities came easily to him in speech, he wore bright gems on his fingers, but whenever he looked in her direction a mask of tenderness was set suddenly on his eyes. The middle morning was coming now hot through the window, and Coppelia stood up to open the glass. She thought of the limberness and ease in Mr. Dooley's subtle bone that endowed him, doubtless, with more youth than he possessed. Every movement she made now borrowed poise from the Englishman's culture; she moved, pure as a figure on a vase, stirred by each movement, to the window opening out upon the road.

When she touched the wood her gestures fell from her, broke off sharply from leg and arm, and dropped in pieces. There below on the edge was Mr. Dooley walking by, so near she might have whispered his name and he would have heard it. The blood ran up in her face, and she waited, breathless and shaken, to see if he would turn to their door. His pace was languid, as though the morning's torpor had beset him: his feet in their dove-gray suede were loitering in the dust. If he lifted his eyes to her, she knew that she too would be stricken. She could no longer bear in silence the implication of his bold sweet glance.

But now she saw that he was not alone; there was a young man following close behind him, and Mr. Dooley had paused to wait there against the white splendor of other people's porticos and the clear waters of the bay.

"Oh, do look down there," said Mr. Dooley, sweeping his cane out towards the sea. The young man had gained the crest and stood in the dust beside him. "Isn't it a poem?" Mr. Dooley said.

"No, just a jingle," said the young man's voice. He passed his hand over his locks, smoothing back his hair. "Just a bit of doggerel," he said.

Mr. Dooley's fresh laughter sounded out.

"Well, then, I'll give you something else," said Mr. Dooley in delight. "Do you see that cloud over there, that very little one like a face on a coin?"

"Yes," said the young man as though in weariness, and he dropped his hand on his hip.

"Well," said Mr. Dooley with a gracious gesture, "I give you that."

"Can you spare it?" said the young man. But Mr. Dooley was looking intently at his face.

"I say," said Mr. Dooley, "did any one ever tell you how really Greek, how truly Grecian you are?" His hand in its chamois glove fell lightly on the young gentleman's arm. "A sculptor would go mad at the sight of you," said Mr. Dooley wildly. He ran his tongue out along his lip. "That splendid head," he said, "set like that on your neck and shoulders."

Coppelia closed the window and sat down. She felt thin and wasted with thirst and hunger; surely the flesh had dropped from her bones and her hair gone white on her head. The thing she had seen in Mr. Dooley's face, she had no name for it. Her mind was spinning in terror in her skull; she could feel the minute steps of its frenzy. Only the corridors to her hearing remained cold and endless, and there Mr. Dooley's words glided singly from door to door, rapped loudly but never entered in. The words he had made a gift of to her had counterpart in other metal; he had forged their likeness from the genuine gold and spent them freely here and there.

She filled her inking pen and set the T-square steady. The first line she touched sent a black river of ink down the length of the drawing.

"It's ruined now," she said. "Now it's ruined."

She looked sharply across the studio to see if father had sensed disaster from where he lay. But his eyes were staring out to sea, his gaze motionless and strong as a beam of light turned out upon the water. Coppelia lifted the bottle of evil ink and emptied it upon the board; it fell like a blot on the temple; it ran like tar over every stone and blotted the whole of it out. Then she crossed the room and sat down by her father. Here no roofs intervened, no roadside menaced. She sat down in the little chair beside him where she might follow the direction of his eyes out over the sea.

"I've ruined the drawing," she said. "The ink spilled all over it. I don't know how it happened."

His eyes were opened on her, hard and upbraiding, but without suspicion. She laid her soft bare arm along the length of his and touched his fingers, servile, like a fallen woman returned to his just anger. She felt no pity for him, but greed for the strength that fortified his body. Then let me return to you, father, she said in her heart. Let me come back to you, submissive to your ends. She pressed close against him whispering to his great fleshy ear, I can begin again, father. Wooing his wrath aside, courting his patience, with the grin on her face strapped tight like a burden to carry.

PETER FOXE

Peter Foxe had a skin clear and fresh as a girl's, but a thick raw look in his bones such as a German youth might have. But that he came from England the native people knew very well, and even the other people eating then at the Gasthaus at the crossroads knew it in spite of the native-like pack on his shoulders, and his knees and a good piece of his thighs out, coarse and bare. Many things about him said as much: the swell of his skull high at the back and the thickness and length of his hair, or else the shy faded look in his eyes that study or wonder maybe had cast in a veil before him. And when he opened his mouth at table, it was enough. He could not speak the language well at all.

It was the summertime and the fields were full of it. The air was pure, and the mountaintops ablaze with snow, with some of the clear bright elegance of their breath given to the lower places. It was warm enough, but ready in the shadow or in the middle afternoon to alter. In the dining hall of the Gasthaus, the sun through the glass parched with thirst anyone sitting in the mountain place. There at the table, Peter Foxe could see the glacier fair and far, as if painted in miniature on the window pane.

To be born in England opened such places like history to a man; parted other countries intimate and wide, and made the mountains of them as familiar as the back hills of any English county. Austria was not a voyage to him any more, once having become a place for walking every August. In that yearly summer holiday Peter Foxe had learned the paths up and the cuts down, and the huts to sleep in, and the places where avalanches might crack suddenly in devastation, bloodless and faceless, and inno-cent-seeming as the icing on a cake; year after year taking the same passes, or with variations in descent and ascent until he knew the region between Milan and Salzburg like a cultivated garden.

Outside the people were passing by in the dust, or else those who were weary pausing in the shade of the fir trees, but all, from whatever country, with the air drawing and arming them. However sore their eyes might have been for the look of a glacier, or for the sight of the mountains sliding down the other side, it would all have come to nothing if the air had not enriched them with strength and given them even a nobility. And now, as if it were the custom and no one surprised at the spectacle, he saw a tall woman in a dress, unlike the other women in their breeches, come along the edge of the road with two children following by her, and walking in their midst a coarse-haired little white beast untethered and flowers wound on the horns and laid around the bony brow.

Sitting there in the dining room of the Gasthaus waiting for the cheese and the confiture, Peter Foxe watched them passing: the woman with light braids pinned high on her head, a crown of hair regally borne, and the two children. The boy wore Tyrol breeches and green braces with

edelweiss embroidered on them, and the little girl walked
with her hand laid on the white goat's tasseled spine. The
short tail wagged like a rabbit's tip, hastily up and down,
and then in a moment they had all gone past the window
and out of his sight, the woman and the two children with
the goat in their midst walking slowly and peacefully
towards the fields and the stream and the sun, and towards
the sudden inescapable end of the town.

He would go that way himself after eating, and before it
was fairly evening he would be on the glacier. It was not
the first time he had come here, and he knew that he too
would take the fields, deep-grassed and starred with
flowers, instead of the road, for the road came to an end at
the end of the houses and the fields ran on unbroken until
the climb began. Summer after summer he had passed
here, and every year his chastity was still there in his face,
untouched. In a little while he would be twenty and then
something would have to be done about women. But the
freshness, the callowness, the slumber before the pollen is
gone was on his features, not yet blown off forever by
familiarity with women. But now it was enough: the sharp
printless crust of the glacier scaled time and again, scaled
and left unaltered as only things of relentless power could
remain unscathed. When he went out the door of the
Gasthaus, the golden hairs on his bare arms sprang
upright at the touch of the mountain breeze, in some
strange nameless wonder that he thought must be like to
love.

He did not see the woman and the two children again
until his feet were already treading the grass of the
meadows, but the thought of them was somewhere in his
mind. Then he saw them ahead, moving against the

beginning of the wood; the woman walking tall and even, moving almost voluptuously and without haste, and the children and the white goat, sometimes before her and other times lingering behind. Far and above were the aquamarine, bottomless blue fissures gashed in the snow-like ice, gaseous green and blue. There would be the veins spread fine and treacherous as wire, surface to the slow covert boiling of the earth beneath; there would be the ice peaks standing separate or in company lifted out of the slowly breaking, the immovable burden, of the glacier's imperceptible descent. The mountains rising, and the glacier foaming in hard slopes from the black dripping snout of ice and above, the séracs horning out in warning, these, in any month, were the best season of the year.

Peter Foxe came to the stream, and there he took the pack from his shoulders. He sat down and unlaced his thick boots with his finger. The grass was fresh and short and dark as emeralds here, and the mountain flowers stood forth brightly against the mat of grass. The woman and the children and the white goat crowned with flowers had moved on to other places; but he remembered the woman. He thought of love, not of the touch and indecency of it, but of the great things it promised and brought men to do. There was a crowning, a mysterious gift in women that had never been given. He saw it borne with dignity, and with-held, in the flesh of wives, and in handsome women passing. He sat so, remembering the tall woman, with his naked feet laid on the stones in the scattered water of the stream. The anguish of the water's cold spread blue and aching up his white strong continent legs.

In a half hour, it might be, he would start the ascent, but now the heat of the hour and the lunch he had eaten

were heavy on him. He sat with his head lowered, and soft
in his neck he suddenly felt it: the cool stirring breath of a
living creature. He could not turn to see, nor wished to,
for the strange sweet languor that beset him. His heart
was filled with pleasure, but still he would not move to see.

After a while, when the breath and the lip even of the
loving stepless thing seemed lying in embrace on his neck,
he turned his head swiftly in passion. And then he saw the
crown of flowers, and the goat's unflickering ear, and the
fringe of white hair, like a child's fringe, cut evenly across
its brow. He turned completely on his thighs, and the goat
did not take fright, but shifted its chin nervously in haste.
Peter Foxe saw the ankles perishable as twigs, and the
rosy, nippled bag hanging fresh and clean between the
goat's hind legs.

"Oh, goat, goat," said Peter Foxe softly, and he put out
his hand to stroke the children's goat, but at this she went
off again over the grass, her mouth set, her yellow eye
edged with lash, and her ears laid back among the flowers
on her head. He saw that her horns were young and girlish
still, as delicate as a crescent moon set lightly on her skull.

He watched her make her way into the needled woods,
and then the woman and the two children came down on
the other side of the water and surprised him sitting there.
The woman saw him first and stopped short at the stream;
between them flowed the shallow diffused melting of the
glacier's strength.

"*Grüssgott,*" said the woman. The two children stood
still with their brows lowered, looking up at Peter Foxe
from under. But the sight of the woman so close now had
sent language from his thoughts like the wings of a dove
and he could not answer her greeting.

"Look at his bare feet," said the little boy, and when the children started to laugh Peter Foxe stood up and said:

"I'm English too."

He saw the woman's sad eager face alter. "Oh, English," she said, speaking her own tongue in relief to him. "English," and a light seemed to have fallen willingly on her brooding face. "I've been so long here without hearing a word of English."

For him it might have ended there and there would have been no more to it. But the woman had been longer alone than a woman can bear to be. He heard her voice, but the words came and went with little meaning in them. He saw her standing, tall and noble, with the water spread out fan-like in between them.

"You're out here on a vacation, I suppose?" she said.

"Yes," said Peter Foxe. "Yes. I'm on vacation."

"It's all very well for you, for young men like you," she said, "just coming out here for a week or two for vacation. But I've had two months in this place without hearing a word of my own language. I've had far and away enough."

Peter Foxe stood still on his bare feet, listening. He looked into her fair grieving face, but there seemed no words to say in comfort. Her voice was the voice of anyone at all from England, but her flesh in this lost place was beautiful and divine with the marvelous mystery in it still withheld.

"It's unpleasant, you know," she said. "It isn't as if I had any grown people with me. The children are in bed by six, and the evenings, week after week, with nothing, nothing. It's really a bit thick, you know."

Peter Foxe felt his voice gone parched and hard in his throat, but the sound of it came to him.

"You have very pretty little children," he heard it say.

"Yes, yes, oh, of course," said the woman, putting the hair back from the little boy's brow. "The Carlisles, you know. Good family. I've always had places with good families."

"Oh, they're not your children?" said Peter Foxe. His woolen stocking hung useless in his hand, and the blood of his confusion ran burning to his hair.

"Oh, no, not mine! I say!" The Englishwoman stood there laughing, holding a hand of each child in her own white hands. But it was certain she had spoken in reproof to him; because of his reverence for her he had not seen at all how young she felt herself to be.

"Oh, now, I didn't mean *that!*" said Peter Foxe.

"Mean what?" said the Englishwoman. When he looked into her face now, the look of it startled the blood in his head; it had nothing to do with the random of the words she spoke; it was lifted, and the lips parted as if in thirst, and the high color waiting like fruit for the mouth below her wooing eyes.

"You're from Lancashire, aren't you?" she said, speaking softly.

"Aye. From Bury," said Peter Foxe, hoarse and humbled with shyness on the other side of the stream.

"Are you going over the glacier?" she said, holding the children's hands in hers.

"Yes," said Peter Foxe. "I'm going over it."

"Tonight?" said the woman slowly.

"Yes. I'm on my way now," said Peter Foxe. He stood there, bewildered, like a man gone blind and speaking painfully from his affliction. "I'm meeting friends, some boys from school. We'll sleep in the hut and go down the other side tomorrow."

Suddenly the Englishwoman sat down, settled hope-lessly in the grass on the opposite side and arranged her skirts beneath her. As she leaned forward, he saw the opening in her blouse, and the fair mysterious flesh that parted there. Even through the widths and breadths of her skirts he could see the outline of her body, and now that she was seated and the hem drawn back, the legs crossed over and curved firmly in her stockings.

"It's all very well for you young men," she said. "Here today and gone tomorrow and no one to account to." Her eyes were fixed in bitterness on him. "You can sleep wherever you will and how, and no questions asked." Her voice had no insinuation in it, but now he saw her body stir in her skirts as though she were arousing languorously from sleep. The children had disappeared, moving from flower to flower toward the wood.

"Why don't you come and sit on this side of the stream for a little while?" the Englishwoman said.

The strength had gone from his legs, and Peter Foxe dropped down on the grass. He began to pull his stockings on, drawing them quickly over his naked feet, moving furtively, in fear. When he looked up again, the woman's eyes were on him still.

"I'll have to be getting on now if I want to reach the hut before dark," he said.

She had drawn her skirts tighter and more divulgent across her womanly knees, and now her features were no longer visible in his swimming sight. Only this deep and purposeful rod of dynastic right seemed wielded in her gaze.

"You're young to be seeing the world alone," she said, and her voice lingered soft and warm as a bare arm thrown about him. His fingers were stricken and fell to trembling over the leather thongs of his boots. "But you're a fine big lad," she said. "Which way did you come up the valley?"

"I came on foot from Bolzano," said Peter Foxe, but the blood was reeling in his body. His head was down and his forefinger hooked the lacings tighter.

"You must be strong then," said the woman. "That's what I like about our people." He could not lift his head, but he heard her rise from the grass and start towards the shallow water. Her voice was coming closer, as though she were already crossing from stone to stone. "It must be very nice for you," she was saying, *nice*, with a gleam of savagery in her tone, "it must be nice to be a man, strong and free, free as the wind, with nothing to fear, taking what you want whenever you want it, and no regrets, going on just the same after, gay as a lark. . . ."

Peter Foxe stood up quickly and made as if to reach for his pack, but his eyes were smitten then by the overbearing rod in the woman's strong suave gaze. She stood still in the middle of the stream and he watched the smile that took shape like an insult on her mouth.

"Don't be afraid," she said. "If you were a gentleman you'd put out your hand and help me over. I've as much right as you to come to the other side."

He saw her swaying, soft and impelling, her flesh warm and as if mutilated by the shadows of the trees' arms, and her hand out, but even before her words had died on the air the sobbing and moaning in the woods behind Peter Foxe had begun. The sound ran over the woman's face and left it haggard. Her hands clasped in terror on her breast as though to wring succor from its full soft shape.

"The children! It's the children!" she said.

Peter Foxe stood rooted at the water's side, harking to

the strange grievous moaning, and only the children's voices piercing out at last sent him running to the wood and wildly through the trunks of the trees. He searched like a man gone mad, with what might have been the wind in his ears screaming, tearing and crashing in frenzy, but drawn by the secret threads of truth to the terrible heart of anguish. There it lay in the wood, dripping and revealed: the white goat on the moss, with a dog at it; the narrow strong shoulders of a dog bearing the evil sluicing dog-jaws forward, and the fangs bared and ripping at the coarse shaggy hide.

He saw these things swiftly: the children pale as anemones crying out behind a tree together, and even the purity and patience of the goat's head rearing up from pain; even the yellow sad mercy of its eye, and the front legs crooked and delicate, believing still that for their beauty there was some escape.

He did not wait to see but saw these things in the very instant that he ceased to run and brought his boot hard and vicious under the dog's lifted tail. But the man might batter and kick, but still the dog would have his last drop of ecstasy. In the lusting and the taste of blood, recoil and all sensation apart had long been blasted out. The great tempest of the dog's rage had risen and was blowing through his nearly unconscious flesh. There were his teeth, pure white and beautiful, tearing like silk the rosy udders between the goat's stricken legs.

The dog was a wolf, so it seemed to Peter Foxe; tall-leggéd as the goat herself, but with a thin limber body that a man could clasp and bend double in his arms. He tore back the ears in fury and hit the dog's muzzle with the knuckles of his hand. Then he saw the tongue loll out, thick and pointed like a wolf's tongue, and the yelp issue. The goat rose slightly, as if on broken wings, and veered forward on her bent knees a little way.

The dog was off, quick with fright and pain now, panting and whimpering in flight through the trees. And Peter Foxe ran to the goat where she lay, wise and quiet, almost smiling. The blood was coming slowly from her wounds, but she was saved now, she could be healed, and he picked her up, crouched there on his legs, and held her close and tender in his arms. Her head with the flowers fallen sideways lay underneath his chin, sweet and moving as a girl's head might settle and rest in its accustomed place. He held her soft quaking body to him, the long limbs, the small-hoofed powerless feet. His face lay close on the coarse tasteless hair on her forehead, and he could hear the pulse in her quivering flesh falling steadily, flake by flake, as cool as falling snow. So would a young girl lie, he thought, faint and still as the first stars.

"Oh, the brute, the brute!" cried the Englishwoman. She caught up the children's hands and cried out bitterly after the fleeing dog. "Scat, get along there, you brute!" she shouted.

Peter Foxe looked up from the goat's pale, tilted face and spoke sharply to the children's governess.

"Hey, get me my first aid, and the bottle of iodine out of my pack! Quick!"

CONVALESCENCE

All the children came into the room and looked at mother lying on the bed. The four of them stood still, just inside the doorway and looked at her. She might have been dead, so strange she seemed to them, and her mouth never opened to bid or greet them. But father had said they should go up alone to see her, for a grown person might set her to weeping, and it was better that way.

"What is it that makes her weep?" said Bindy.

"It's something to do with her nerves," said father.

"I didn't know people could be sick all summer," Bindy said.

Up they went to her room, and they might have stood so within the door forever had not the wind suddenly sprung to life and flung it closed behind them. There they were, caught in the room with her, and no way to turn. The grass blinds were fanning the sunlight in the windows. Bindy said: "Hello."

"Hello," said mother softly. And then she called out, as though in fear: "Oh, Bindy!" He dropped the hands of the others and went running to her side. She lifted her quivering arm from the bed and put it around him. He

could almost make out the green nightgown in the dim
room, and her rings, and her hair brushed back behind
her ears.

"Oh, Bindy," said mother in her soft fearful voice.
"Look at mother's fingers! Her rings are all too big for
her now!"

"You're not really his mother," said Anne. She spun
around on one foot in the room, elated by the burden of
disaster on the air. "Only Rolly and Midge belong to
you," she said, spinning. Her braids swung out like two
accusing fingers as she spun. Anne and Midge began to
laugh together, the two of them covering their mouths to
muffle their laughter in their hands. The wondrous sense
of infliction set them to tittering and wavering in their
little skirts in the darkened room. But mother had been ill
too long; she had no patience left for them. The stone
hearts of little girls belonged, like those of perverts, in a
privy world of their own.

Rolly was gone from sight, under the bed on his hands
and knees, and no one gave a thought to him. Mother held
Bindy's fingers tight. And "what am I going to do,
Bindy?" she whispered. "I haven't any friends left. Nobody cares any more."

"I'm your friend," said Bindy. He felt her arm pressing
soft around him. "I'm a good friend of yours," he said.

"But I've got so old," said mother in complaint. "The
color's all gone out of my eyes, you know, Bindy. They
won't give me a looking glass. They don't want me to see."

"Do your nerves hurt you very bad?" said Bindy.

"Oh, they hurt awfully, awfully," said mother, and her
voice went suddenly blind with tears. The thought of
herself so grieving, so gentle, defenseless as no other

woman had ever been because of her beauty and her
frailties; such thought returned like a specter to her mind
and moved unseen from one fount of pity to the next. "It
hurts the worst right here, Bindy," she said, and her throat
was parched with anguish. "Put your hand right here
where mother's heart is and maybe you'll help it to go
away."

Bindy put his hand down on her nightdress. He could
feel the soft quivering life of her heart in protest, as
though he held it captive in his hand.

"There're an awful lot of kinds of sickness, aren't
there?" said Bindy.

"This kind has made me so old," said mother, whispering in sorrow to him. "I know what my eyes are like, and
my hair coming out in handfuls all over my head, Bindy."

"I bet you'd get a prize anywhere," said Bindy. He
could not bear the tears to run down her face. "I'm not
fooling. I bet you'd get a prize almost anywhere for being
the most beautiful woman."

Mother lifted her head up, strong from the pillow.

"Bindy, honey, do you want to do something for
mother?" she said. "Just get me my looking glass over
there, so I can have a little peek at myself."

But the little girls had sped across the room to be the
first at the dressing table. There they stood, touching one
thing and then another, puzzled that they could not find it
there.

"There isn't any looking glass any more," said Anne.

"They've taken everything," mother cried out.
"They've taken mother's little curved scissors, and even
her nail file, Bindy! They've taken everything that hurts
as if they thought I'd hurt myself some more!"

It was then that father came in and took the hands of the little girls.

"You must come away now," he said, and he looked shyly and uncertainly at mother. "Long enough for the first time, children," said father. "Come, Bindy, son," he said. "Mother must have a rest."

Father leaned over to kiss mother's face, but she turned it sharply on the pillow.

"Oh, don't! Oh, don't!" she said in her weak grievous voice. "I'm so tired, so tired."

They went out the door with him, the two little girls and Bindy. Father closed it softly behind, and they all went soundlessly down the stairs. In a moment mother began to cry; she lay crying senselessly, weakly into her pillow. After a while, with the tears still wet on her face, she fell asleep.

A wonderful fresh darkness had come into every part of the room while she lay sleeping. When she opened her eyes, it was deep behind the chairs in the room, and hanging like a cloth flung over the table. The highboy in the corner had a row of light brass smiles, and somewhere within the shadows was a presence. There was no sound, but she could feel its breath and its being.

"Who's in this room with me?" she said. A dew of terror had sprung out on her brow, but she spoke the words sharp and loud across the room. She could not move, but she watched the little man stand up beside her. He put out his hand to her on the bed.

"Rolly," he said, with his head cocked.

"Oh, Rolly, Rolly," breathed mother. "Oh, Rolly." But her bare limbs were shaking with cold in the sheets. "How ever did mother's baby . . ." she said, and her teeth were shaking together. It must be the heart of winter, and she would never be warm again. "Does little Rolly want to help mother?" she said softly. "Come here, Rolly, darling," she said, "and mother will tell you what to do."

The little man came close in the darkness and she seized his hand in her fingers. He seemed like a dwarf to her, twisted and weird, with his face unseen in the gloom. "Rolly," she whispered, "now Rolly only needs to walk over to mother's bureau. You see mother's big bureau? Now just walk sweetly over to mother's big bureau and open the drawer wide." She gave him a little push with her fingers, and he sat down suddenly on the floor. "Rolly," said mother. "Rolly, dear, get up." She could not lift herself from the pillows to see. "Rolly," she said, "you don't want to make mother sad, do you? You want to do what mother tells you to do." She felt the hand of ice on her heart, and she could not shake it from her. The little man stood up in the dark, and what time of life does sense begin to come to them, she thought wildly. Is it at two years of age or three that they run and do as they are bid? "Rolly," she said, "now you want to help mother, don't you? Now run quick, quick to mother's big bureau and do just as she tells you."

Suddenly Rolly drew away in the darkness, and set off towards the window. She reared up her head on her neck, like an adder watching, peering helpless, cold, into the room that the night was blotting away. She heard Rolly strike a chair in the dark, and his voice cry out in pain.

"Oh, Rolly," said mother. "Aren't you mother's big Rolly? It didn't hurt so very much, did it now, Rolly? You're not going to cry over a silly thing like that. You must be mother's big brave boy and pick yourself up and do what she tells you."

She heard him sniff and move on the floor.

"Rolly," she whispered, with her head raised, seeking. "Rolly, where are you now?"

His hand slapped the smooth side of a wooden body.

"Here," said Rolly's small voice out of the dark.

"Yes, yes," said mother softly. "Now, pull the drawer open, Rolly." Her breath went whistling through her teeth as they chattered. She could hear the bureau drawer slowly easing wide.

"Rolly dear," said mother, "just put your little hand right down inside it, right down inside, right there next to the window where you are."

She could hear Rolly grunt as he groped in the darkness, and suddenly the door opened and the nurse walked straight into the room. Mother lay still on the bed and watched the nurse switch on the small blue light in the corner. Her apron hung down from her waist, as blank as paper. When she turned around she saw the baby staring at the light.

"So this is where Rolly's been all the time!" she said.

"I've been asleep," said mother in her soft weary voice. "I didn't even know."

The nurse took him up in her arms and he did not speak nor turn his head towards the deep wide bed. She bore him out the door and left it standing wide. Mother could hear her going down the hall, down, down, down the three little steps to the nursery. In a moment she would hear the water spilling warm into the bath.

The children came up the front stairs, quietly, on their toes, as father had told them they must walk now: Bindy, and Midge, and Anne passing down the hall. Mother knew the sound of each footfall as though it were a separate hammer striking. Single and blind the blows fell on her flesh, summoning her anguish from repose, striking row upon row of brass-eyed nails into the lid that closed upon exhaustion.

"Bindy," she cried out from her room. "Just Bindy. Come and see mother."

She turned her head to watch his slight, muted body come in from the hallway. Midge and Anne went whispering away.

"Bindy," she said, borrowing ease from some other time and place. "Bindy, will you get mother something out of her bureau drawer."

He stood still for a moment, slim and shy, looking at her.

"You're getting better, aren't you?" he said.

"I'm trying hard to get better," she said, curbing the wild speed of her blood. "Oh, so hard!" If he did not make haste, the nurse might come back to the room. "Bindy, dear, just put your hand down in the corner of the drawer that's open." Bindy set down his net of shining glassy marble eyes and crossed the soft dim room.

"There's a little bottle in there, Bindy darling," said mother. "Do you find it, darling, underneath the handkerchiefs and things?"

"Yes," said Bindy. He took it out of the drawer and held it up. "It's a pretty big bottle," he said.

"That's the one, Bindy, that's it," said mother. Her hand was shaking out before her. "Now give it to me, darling." He brought it across the room to her, treading soft and careful on the matting. She reached out her own stricken hand. "It's just between you and me, isn't it, Bindy? You and I will have a secret, you see, and we won't tell nurse or daddy or anyone at all."

"All right," said Bindy. He picked up his marbles. "Maybe if you're getting better I could play marbles here?" he said.

"But your bath must be ready now," said mother. "You'd better go now, Bindy. You'd better go and see."

She held up her head, listening to his fading steps and the hop and the skip at the nursery steps, going down. Then she set her teeth hard into the cork, and out it eased with a slow sucking gasp. Her arm was quaking in the shaded light, but she tilted the bottle up and the dark rich whiskey ran scalding down. At the first taste of it, the cold went off; she could feel it floating off, like veils from her limbs, as the cold had always done. A queer heathen laughter was beginning to shake within; the stuff ran thin against the bottle's glass and burned its way deeper and deeper into her swooning flesh.

When the nursery door opened, she flashed the bottle under the cover. But the nurse's step went past the open door and halted at the linen closet in the hall. Mother heard her taking the towels out for the children's bath. Everything was soft and safe; the terror had been struck away, like shackles, from her wrists. Outside in the summery evening she could hear father pacing the walk below. Up and down went his steps, as if there were some distress in his soul. Up and down, walking his unrest to sleep, as if to ease its storming. What does he fear, what does he fear, thought mother, and she was shaken all over with laughter. What does he fear now that the winter has given over to spring?

After a while the little girls came down the hall, borne gently on an odorous warm wave from the bath. She could remember the smell of the powder on their flesh, and their hair brushed shining. She lay still in the swinging circles of the bed, seeking the highboy's smile, or flower in curtain for anchor, and listening, whether she would or no, to the little girls' soft voices. This was the place allotted the grown, she thought: to eavesdrop, to watch, to spy.

"You're not my *real* sister," Anne's voice was saying. Spy on their actions, their hands, and the drop of their skirts; spy on their talk together. The warmth of the night was beating softly, softly now onto the dark shoals of the room.

"Who am I?" said Midge, hushed in wonder. "Who am I?"

The rising sea of warmth was lapping close to the bed now.

"Bindy's not your *real* brother," said Anne. "Father was married two times. Father's not your father. Bindy and father belong all to me."

"Who am I?" said Midge, lifting her voice in wonder to wisdom. Maybe these words were the words they spoke every day to each other, in worship of the mystery, or maybe they had never spoken them before.

"I don't know who you are," said the wise voice over the open sea of darkness. "Father's not your father."

The dark tide was full now, had risen; mother could no longer stir for the weight of it creeping warm upon her flesh. She was rocked close, cradled and quiet in it.

"Where's my father?" said Midge, stopped still forever in wonder.

"Your father's dead," Anne's voice said. There was a wondrous murmur of sound now as though Bindy and Rolly too had set sail on the creeping waters.

"Did they kill him with a knife?" said Midge. Mother could hear the paddling of the oars come close, and the keels approaching. In a moment the prows would be on her, but still she did not stir. She lay floating, her arms out, her head back, drifting.

"Give me your hand, Rolly," said Bindy. He spoke in a hard whisper across the waters.

"I don't know," said Anne. "Maybe they cut his head off." The little girls tittered with laughter. "Or maybe he was sick and died in bed like everybody."

"Maybe mother will die," said Midge.

"You fools!" whispered Bindy. "Rolly, give me your hand going downstairs."

THE FIRST LOVER

For over a month the music of their conversation had been gently rocking the *pension* to sleep. Out of the window behind their three fair heads rose the rocky hills of Beausoleil, so covered with little pink villas, with porcelain cats, and china turtles that the dignity of a bare rock rearing ugly as sin between the houses was enough to make the heart stand still. The three girls themselves were out of their own country with an elation signifying that everything that tasted unpleasant had been left behind. Such beautiful meals they were given in the *pension*, such fine things to eat, and the sunshine every day as lavish as rain.

This was a vacation time for them. This was the miracle of repose their father had given them for a little while. They filled it with rich excursions, hot chocolate in the afternoon and cakes, and with such a wealth of conversation with mere acquaintances, but still it was in their faces that they could not forget. They could not forget the lean years that lay behind them and, if they were young, still they had lived long enough to remember what the years and the times had done to their father. Professor Albatross and his fiery heart had been extinguished. Their father

had become an old man. It was only at certain sentimental
hours now that they could write to him with open hearts in
the same way that they had been accustomed to run to him
to dry their tears in the hairs of his beard.

This was what they recounted with their pure faces and
their continuous letter-writing, and with their conversation about other things. If the eldest girl would look out of
the window and say, *"Aber* father would certainly never
have played chess after lunch on a day like this; he would
have liked sitting in the casino gardens, especially now
that they've changed the flowers again," this was a sign for
the three of them to sit in silence after the first words of
understanding had been spoken. "Father. Ah, yes. Father.
Jah." And the younger one would turn her handkerchief in
her fingers. It was easy to see from what they said that
they had all loved their father very much.

When the Englishman stepped into the dining room one
day at noon, surely the first thoughts of the three German
girls must have turned to Professor Albatross. Here was a
man about whom their father would have nodded to them
in a concert hall if he had walked into it. Such a handsome
man must surely have caught father's attention, and he
would have looked from one to the other of them, beating
his head as if to the sound of music and smiling.

When first he set foot in the room something sprang to
life in every corner of it. The sight of this strange young
man standing there made the three cradles of the German
girls' voices upset. Not even an *"ach"* nor an *"aber"* to
meet the occasion. "An Englishman," they exchanged
among them. The fresh, the sturdy, the golden cousin-
ness of all gallant England filled them with dismay.

"Oh, I say . . ." remarked the young Englishman. He

had looked carefully at every little piece of the room. "I wanted a table," he said. And the old lady gave him one in a minute or two.

But while he was waiting every one had a chance to see it: the way his hair grew up and how his elegant head turned on his neck. He held his chin high, and his eyes were as blindly blue as if they had been extinguished with a red-hot iron. All the sun of the coast had seemingly descended upon his cranium and was dripping down over his brows. Little rays of it marched across the backs of his hands. Maybe this beauty is the toughest; it is now the purest left in the world, thought the eldest girl. For an Italian must wear a color about his neck or a ring in his ear, but this British beauty depends on nothing at all but fogs that would throttle you if they could and English rains that would not fall in any other place.

The Englishman sat down at the little table they had given him and began to crunch radishes like almonds beneath his teeth. He looked steadily out of the window into the porcelain eyes of the cats and the stony doves which ornamented the garden. It seemed as if he could not bring himself to look into the eyes of the human faces that were in the room with him. The three girls had a glance for every mouthful that passed his lips. When the fresh figs were set before him he ate them in the English way, rippling the skin back until the fig in his hands bloomed open like a flower.

There seemed to be nothing in any part of him that had survived a spectacle of pain. Surely, thought the eldest girl, he had never been beset, and if ever he had been sore in his heart for love or food, he had put that carefully aside. Everything on his plate he took for granted, even the salt in its shaker was the customary thing. He had never been touched at all, she was thinking, nor had he any idea that people sometimes had less or did without.

Everything that had ever happened to them, she would keep to herself. In her bones it would reside, and he would not know that for years they had been like mice lean for a crumb. Not a drop of his blood would ever sound the poverty of the years that ran behind them. They were in a new country of greed and plenty and they would forget, by turning their faces away, they would forget everything that had made their hearts like winter apples.

"Lieblinge," said the eldest girl to her sisters, "we must do our nails and behave like princesses."

They had to drop their lids to cover the jubilation in their eyes. This was the reward they owed Professor Albatross. What a recompense to the old man if his three daughters could between them bear back to him this evidence of health and prosperity, this assurance that all was well. Whether it was the state of his flesh or something else besides that gave the Englishman his temper of wealth and empire, they did not know. But his it was, and merely the sight of it would surely be enough to revive the old man's courage.

When the Englishman had finished eating he dabbed at his mouth with his napkin and then placed it in a little heap by the side of his plate. He had not tied it into a bowknot, as others had done, or made it into a butterfly. He had eaten well, but with such dispatch. He walked out of the dining room with his own standard set relentlessly upon him. He would recognize nothing short of health and austerity. Whatever he stood for had a name, and he would accept nothing less.

He walked directly out into the back garden after lunch, and from their window the three German girls could see him. They stood in their bedroom, behind the folds of the curtains, and relished the rosy backs of his ears and his narrow wrists crossed behind him as he walked. Suddenly he swung about and sat down in a wicker chair, and they started back from the window in fright. But his clear gaze and his short straight nose were pointing off towards Monte Carlo. Surely he did not even know the three girls were there.

A strange sort of defiance for one another was in their eyes, and the eldest knew that it was she herself who must say what was to be said. She turned from the window and picked up her embroidery hoop and its veil of work from the table. The prosperity of this cloth with a fresh skein of white silk to it was equally as far from anything they had ever known. They had never before had time for embroidery until they had come to this affluent land. Beyond the window they could see the Englishman with an ivory part running through his hair. He was reading the *London Times* in the sun, with his legs stretched out before him and his ankles in gray socks crossed like a silver chain. Suddenly the eldest girl ran to her sisters to hide her eyes and her blushes in the soft turn of their shoulders.

"He looks so *well!*" she whispered, and the wind of her breath in their necks made them shriek softly with laughter. "As if he had never been hungry!"

She was laughing, too, but her eyes were crying. She stood before them, laughing, with her small hands covering her face.

He must have seen so many beautiful clothes, she was thinking. There was nothing she could wear that would catch his attention at all. She stood in the room with her two sisters, thinking of how she would speak to him. Not at dinner, for there would be too many people at the tables, but when he would perhaps walk out into the garden after having eaten, and she would throw a little scarf over her shoulders and follow him. In her mind she could hear the sound of her own tentative *"bitte, bitte"* following in his wake. But however she thought of him she could not forget the forbidding set of his jaw when he bit into his bread.

She would make up some kind of a fine story about their lives, which had remained at home while surely he was traveling everywhere. "Your countrymen and you, you are forever traveling for beauty" was one of the things that she would say. She would talk of her father—Baron Albatross; *jah,* why not a baron?—and of the idleness and poetry that had nourished them. With all of Germany suffering in one way or another, she would say to him, it was strange but true that they had never known any suffering at all. It was her father's high position that had protected them. She would say it so many times, over and over, that she would make it true.

"Do you ever come to Munich?" she would ask him.

By the time he came to Munich, she was thinking, by that time he would be in love. By that time his heart would be winged like an archangel, and he would not care if she were rich or poor. And if there were a moment of silence in the garden after dinner, or a pause of any kind between all the things they had to say, she would go on, "My two little sisters are with me. . . ." Suddenly she kissed their faces.

"Oh, don't even mention us to him!" they whispered. "He is to be for you. He is to be your lover. We want him to be yours."

She was thinking that she must carry herself like a rich lady, and that any plaintiveness at all must be kept out of her voice. No prithee, do, please, pray. No insomuch as, but "Indeed, you *must* visit our prosperous city. . . ." "If only I could wear four pairs of earrings at once," she was thinking. She looked at her wan face in the glass.

"I must smile," she said.

She crossed the room to the window to see if he were still sitting in the sun. The newspaper had dropped from his fingers and he was there, reflecting, dreaming, and pondering, deeply meditating. She wondered what dreams were in his head. And then suddenly the Englishman turned and looked up into her face.

If a blush had sought to shame him for his impertinence, it perished in the relentless pride of his race. He lifted one hand to shade his eyes, and then he got to his feet. The German girl was clinging, half-swooning, to the window frame.

The Englishman cleared his throat.

"You're not by any chance . . ." he said, talking up from the garden, "I mean to say, I saw your names on the register a while ago . . . I dare say yours. Are you by any chance daughters of Professor Albatross of Munich? I must have studied with your father—physics—at least, if he is."

"Yes," said the German girl.

Her voice could scarcely be heard. Her fingernails had turned white upon the sill.

"Yes," she said.

Her face was so contorted that her sisters scarcely knew her.

"Professor Albatross," she whispered out of the window. "Yes."

The two sisters saw her face hanging in anguish at the window. They themselves were too stricken to summon a word of response. She was standing with her mouth hanging open. She could not make another sound.

"Fancy running into you here," said the Englishman.

Behind her hung the deathly silence—*grosse Seelen dulden still*—with now and again the whisper of her sisters' breathing like the flight of a mouse across the room. The Englishman was standing with one hand in his pocket, and the other lifted to shade his eyes.

"Fancy," he said. With this he gave a little nod of his head.

"I just stopped off for lunch here," he said.

He smiled up at the German girl in the window, and with this he walked into the house, leaving the three sisters to one another. They turned around upon one another in some kind of fury that had never possessed them before. Their eyes were warm, and their teeth were strung like pearls across their faces. They had so much to say to one another that they didn't know where to begin.

CAREER

The day was quite fair and the ground soft as spring under foot, and the boy and the diviner set off together to walk to the farm. The diviner was a tall man and he had on his face the look of serenity a religious man might wear, because of his belief in something that had covert life, that went strong as wind blowing, and as impervious, underground.

The diviner talked of water passing under a bridge, or passing under a boat, and if he stood on a bridge or stepped in the boat this water's flowing did not change the beating of his heart. But if he went into a house and water was passing unbeknown under it, his pulse told him this. The boy was so new to the work that everything the man said had a sound of wonder. The man said he had a friend who built a house and slept in a front room of it, and day after day his health faded and the doctors could find no reason why it should be so.

"When I went to see him," said the diviner, walking the road with the boy and chewing at a bit of grass between his teeth, "I saw his face and then I knew what it was. It was water."

"Was there water passing by the house?" said the boy quickly, and the man shook his head.

111

"Water going by means nothing," he said. "It's water running under the ground that counts. There was water running under the house on the side he slept on, but nobody knew anything about it. He couldn't get any rest at night and his appetite left him. Most people are dead to it," said the diviner. "But this man, he might have died. When I came into the room where he was the hair stood right up straight on my head, and the ends of my fingers started tingling. I knew what it was then and I took hold of his hand. But he had to let go of me and sit down because his heart was beating more than he could stand."

The boy listened to everything the man said, for he was setting out in life now; now he was going towards what work would bring him to. It seemed to him that he would have to be shaped thought by thought and bone by bone by whatever career he undertook, for he had no clear picture in his mind of what kind of a person he was or what he was intended to be. Whether he would be a man like his father, working as a builder, or like men he saw passing in the street or serving in a store, he did not know. But being young, he believed the choice had fallen on him: he said little, but he waited, knowing that the choice was made and that he could not be like the others, saying not a word but listening to the men who talked in his father's house, and to his father, knowing without vanity that he could not become the same.

The diviner himself was three men walking along the road, not one of them paying any heed to the black-faced sheep or the coarse, clay-red, small cattle they passed. He was first a man who lived to himself, and he was a man the engineering people employed as a locator of water, and he was as well a stranger speaking to the new boy as they went along to the farm where water was wanted. January is a warm time in Australia, and the farm was far, and the wet grass by the road was already beginning to stand up towards the sun when it came in sight.

The diviner was saying that the power extended to silver as well as to a twig of hazel he sometimes used, and he took a half crown and a bit of bent wire from his pocket, and, in his hand as they walked, the wire drew straight of itself and reached out as if in hunger towards the piece of silver he had concealed in the palm of his other hand. Whichever way he moved the hand with the half crown in it, the wire changed its course and sought the direction of the silver. The man laughed a little, but still he was pleased by the look of awe in the new boy's face.

The boy stopped still in the road, and was staring, for whatever devotion to something else there was in him had been made impure by church taken as a weekly, dutiful thing. But this miracle he saw was what the miracle of voices singing and the high ribs of stone might have been if they had been kept, like gold, until he was old enough to see. The wire straightening out, like a reed in flowing water, and reaching for the coin was the mystery given a name at last. He stood still in the road, with his mouth open, watching the man put the half crown and the bit of wire back in his pocket again.

"Come along now," said the man. "There's the farm off there where the trees are."

The sky and the sea below the line of land were one now, the same, fresh, loud, unbroken blue as if a wind had cleaned them out. The boy looked down, trying to see and follow the line that lay between them.

"I knew a rock once," he said, "where if you put your

ear down against it you could hear the water running underneath."

"Water doesn't always say which way it's going," the diviner said.

The farm people were in the house when the diviner knocked at the door, and they stopped whatever they were doing, the woman washing dishes and the old man stringing beans by the window, stopped without haste, without interest almost, and asked them at the door if they would have a piece of bread or a drink before setting out over the ground. But the diviner was thinking of the business he had to do, and he said they would take something later when the work was done. There was no reverence or respect in the woman's voice when she spoke to the diviner. She talked of the artesian well they wanted as they all walked out through the garden together, but there was no homage in her manner although the diviner alone had the knowledge of where the well would be.

They went past the rabbit huts, talking; and the boy felt the walk in his legs now, and his mouth was dry. The sun was hot as summer, and he lingered behind in the shade and looked in at the rabbits in their separate nests of hay. They were all of one race, long, limber beasts, brown-coated and sleek, with flecks of yellow at the points of their hairs. He put his hand in quietly through the side of one box where the wire was parted, and the rabbit never stirred in her corner. Only her eye quivered, cool and dark and waking, as he drew his hand down the soft, loose velvet of her hanging ears.

Then he went on quickly after the farm people and the diviner, for this was the work he had to do now, and he must learn it word by word. The work had begun by the diviner taking the bit of fencing wire out of his pocket again and twisting it into the shape of a W. He carried it held out before him a little way, the apex of the letter turned up, and when the boy looked at his face he saw that it was altered: the eyes had given up their sight and the color was faded from under his skin, as if a veil had been drawn across. The farm people followed after him, the old man, and the woman, and her husband who had come up from the fields, not speaking, but still not hushed for any kind of wonder they felt, following him as he went slowly, as if blind, across the unresponding land.

They passed over a road packed hard by the feet of cattle, and they were almost at the tree line along the meadow when suddenly it began. The diviner stopped as if he had been struck, and the first quiverings of declaration went through him; almost at once then, the wild surge of power began giving battle in his hand. There he stood rooted, and the others halted behind him, and the boy's breath went out of him at the sight of the W forcing itself inward and downward against the strong outward and upward warring of the man. He had taken his two hands to it now, and his mouth was shut tight against the onslaught of what this was. His body opposed it, his feet braced on the earth in anguish, and the veins stood out in his arms as if ready to burst through the skin.

The boy had scarcely seen it right when the struggle was over. The man had seemingly bowed to the wire's will, and the apex of the letter was pointing earthward to the magnetic thing that passed them under the soil. The diviner moved off, holding the wire out again before him, but his face was quiet and certain now and he did not go

far, only enough to feel the truth repeated. Step by step he
covered the ground that lay close about, and how ever he
turned, the wire turned in his hands to the chosen place,
unswerving, as if thirsting itself for what ran secretly
below.

It was so new to the boy that he did not know if he were
living or dead, or whether or not there were people
standing there in the open air before him. But when they
began talking, he saw that it was a business to them, even
to the diviner it was a business, as common as the stars
moving or the shadow of the earth falling deeper night
after night on the side of the moon. But still he could not
open his mouth or shut it, but must leave it where it was
until the diviner turned to him in a little while with the
wire held out in his hand.

"Come along now," the diviner said, "we'll have to see
if you have the power."

The boy took hold of the wire in his fingers, and
suddenly the tears started running down his face. He
knew he was not moving his hand, but the wire was
turning, not towards the earth or in any earthward direction, but pointing straight to the center of life and blood
where he had been taught his heart should be.

"Oh, come along now," said the diviner with a laugh,
and the farm people as well began laughing at what they
hoped to see. "Now take it easy," said the diviner, speaking with patience, as if he might be teaching a lad to put a
sole on a boot or plane a piece of timber. "Wipe your face
now and take hold of my hand. That'll fix it."

The boy wiped his nose with the back of his hand, and
the diviner reached out and took hold of one end of the
wire. He was holding the boy's spare hand in his, and

before either of them could draw a breath the might of the water struck them. The boy went down under it, thrown as if from the back of a horse, flat on his back, with his mind wiped out for whatever next would come.

It is warm at this time of year in Australia, and the memory of the cold is something that happened at some-time when the continent was taking shape. They set out from it in the glacial time as penguins do from a breaking coastline in the spring, and for warmth they had drawn the Gulf Stream like a scarf around them.

"We were more than an hour on the road," the diviner said. "Can you fetch him some water from the house?" — as if this was any explanation.

TO THE PURE

"Hullo," said the Contessa sitting up straight and cool as an April shower behind the table of cups and cake. She waved her hand toward the new young man. "Come over and have a cup of tea," she said.

New is such a beautiful word, thought the Contessa as the young man made his way across the crowded room to her. It is spelled out of the wind's three best directions: north, east, and west. The thought of them was enough to bring the color flying to her cheeks.

But such big hats were the grand people in Rome wearing this season that the Contessa lost the new young man's face for moments at a time behind them. When she found him again he had halted in confusion before the impossible barrier of Mrs. Whatshername's backside.

"Come on!" called the gay young Contessa. "You've almost made it!"

As he came toward her, she could not tell which he was quite. No matter how much she looked at him, up and down, or gave ear to the tenor of his voice, could she tell. The suspicion lay in the way his toes had of treading the carpet, came fluttering through the tide of conversation, bearing the sweet burden of his body to her chair. But every one, everywhere, so ready to make high-handed decisions; he's this, he's that, about the prophets themselves. He looks like a nice enough young man to me, thought the Contessa.

He wore a little gold chain around one wrist, and he shook it delicately as he leaned over her hand.

"You really are," said the new young man, "the most beautiful woman in Italy. Every one told me you were going to be."

The Contessa gave a snort of laughter.

"What do you know about Italy, young man?" she said. "Sit down. If you've never poked around the hills and seen the women washing their clothes clean in the streams, or seen them carrying their pails on their heads with an indolence I'd give my eyes for! Lemon or milk?" said the Contessa.

She saw that he had been educated with the Jesuits for a scapular showed through his fine silk shirt. As she passed him the platter of sandwiches she put her fingertip on it, her painted nail questioning him like a bloody eye. The young man thrust one hand inside his bosom and drew out the scapular on its ribbon. Not fish nor fowl, thought the Contessa. Merely a little Scotchman dressed up with a scarf around his neck and a locket tapping at his ankle. This was all that set him apart from any poor little clerk you might pass on the street in Edinburgh. It was the Jesuits, maybe, who had given him a little of something else.

She could picture him standing on the corner of a street with his cane on his hip, looking north, east, and west for a fresh face to revive him. If you walked around the water before noon in any continental garden you would surely come upon him feeding the swans or the goldfish, throwing out crumbs on the water and reclining back on the savage head of his cane. He would be wearing the same blue jacket, and the sandals that revealed his toes. Scarcely a kind word would he have for the swans, or so much as a passing glance for the goldfish, his concern being for the pretty picture he was making against the landscape. The Contessa stopped herself sharply from thinking the worst of him.

"Do tell me what remains of England," she said to him. As if any one could ever tell her what had become of the youth of England, the young blood that used to ride to hounds with her! Not so many years ago at that, thought the Contessa. She bowed to some one across the room and turned to the new young man's answer.

He made a small sour mouth at her, and her eyes flashed over the rim of the cup she held to the sight of her own reflection in the glass. Everything as straight as rain before her: the hair, the brows, the nose, the shoulders. Black as a bog her hair combed off her ears, and in the depths of her eyes a wild harp playing. Two years of Italy and of being courteous to strangers had done a thing or two to her face. It had turned the ends of her mouth up sharply in her cheeks, but no amount of bitter talk, of subterfuge, or foreign places could still the wild harp's playing. Something will happen sometime. Something as cool as watercress will be said.

"I don't think I understand," said the new young man. He was going to turn out like everyone else. She would have to suggest people across the room to him—"you must meet Mrs. Howdoyoucallher"—cry out for succor. And then the young man said:

"I say, you knew Arthur Shaw, didn't you?"

The Contessa set down her cup in its saucer. He had given her no warning.

"Arthur?" she said in a moment. She looked brightly at the new young man. Every breath of air in the room had been used so many times over that she could no longer draw it in and out.

"It was Arthur who told me to come and see you," said the new young man. He was tapping a cigarette out of his case.

"So many people," she said aloud to him. "I almost perish every time. Before I married, you know, I was accustomed to the open, the hills, horseback." She seized a cigarette wildly from the young man's case. "I can't tell you what a difference. Complete reversal of all my habits, ways, food, air. Ye know, I used often to walk twenty miles a day and never give a thought to it. What about Arthur?" she said aggressively. "What about him?"

"He's in England, of course," said the new young man.

"Yes," said the Contessa. "Of course, in England. In England of all places! Does he ever come out of England? Ha, ha," she laughed. I made a fine fool of myself over Arthur, she was thinking. "Funny for an Irishman, oh, a real south Irishman, to be heart and soul in England. What do ye think of Arthur yourself?" she said. "It was two years ago I saw him last. Just after I was married. 'Contessa this,' he said, and 'Contessa that' as if he were insulting me. We'd always done our hunting and walking together, and here he was acting like a monkey on a stick. He was an Irishman, if ever there was one," said the Contessa with her eyes shining. "I can't think how he can abide England. Does he live there forever?"

"He likes the background," said the new young man.

"The background!" cried out the Contessa in contempt. "An Irishman! How tired Arthur makes one!" she cried. He came pretty near making a fool of himself over me, she was thinking, however he explains it now. Suddenly the color ran up to her eyes. "Is he still as handsome?" she said.

The new young man looked curiously at her.

"Would you call Arthur a really handsome man?" he said in a minute. Bit by bit he was taking her face apart. He was separating the nose from the eyes, thinning out the grim black brows; the bowls of her temples hollowed out by the side of his glance made her feel singularly a sturdy woman. She had to lift her wrist from the table and eye it, survey her outstretched ankle beneath the table to convince herself that she was still as shapely as a hind.

"Oh, yes," she said coolly. Surely she had known Arthur better than this little puppet ever had. She examined her fingertips. "Without any kind of doubt he was certainly the finest figger of a man I ever saw."

But what in the name of reason might be he like now, after two years of England good and proper? She could see him as he had been, dancing the Spanish fandango, with castanets in his fingers and one of her hats on the side of his head. She could never believe in Ascot any more when she saw his face under it. Everything the brim had stood for, and the yards of lace, had gone under the table with a crash once Arthur had put it on his head.

"I thought he would seem a bit fragile, perhaps," said the new young man. "At least to a woman."

And why to a woman like that, thought the Contessa? A woman, as if it were an object without rhyme or reason, like a giraffe!

"Arthur," she said. She felt the corners of her mouth turning down with the bad taste in it. "I wore him a long time in my *boutonnière*. He smelled so good."

No one had ever withstood her, no one ever. She had letters five trunks deep, but nothing left of Arthur. A bit fragile! After she herself had broken him up like kindling and put him on the logs. Nothing left of him but the way they stood at the end of the hall which embraced so many climates. In the far corners of it were blasts of ice and snow, and down you walked towards the roaring chimney at the heart, out of the glacier, the drifts of cold, the frozen world, into the flowering warmth of the hearth and fire. There they had stood sideways, with one shoulder scorched and the other mottled with gooseflesh, as you do at home in Ireland, with glasses drained of whisky and their hearts beating. Why don't you kiss me, Arthur? she said. Now why did you have to say that? said he. He put his black cape over his shoulders. Now why did ye have to say it? Am I so hideous, she cried, am I such a sight? Would I stop the face of a clock? Would I turn the stomach? No, said Arthur, you wouldn't do any of those things. But you have no understanding of what I am, or you wouldn't ask it of me. You have no understanding of honor. Honor, my eye, she had cried out to him. I've had other men kiss me whether you will or no. Then have them, said Arthur as he went out the door.

"Do you mean to say—" said the new young man. The Contessa came to her senses. She put her cigarette away in the dish.

"I had no idea," he began again. What a shallow little man he was, thought the Contessa in irritation. She saw his face before her; surprised, and thin as water. If ever a thought came through his head, she flattered herself she could have caught it, like a trout, with a bent pin and a passing fancy. Where in the world had a man like Arthur run across him and what speech had they in common?

"I'm only trying to say," said the Contessa impatiently, "that things have been particularly black without him. I never had any principles, and Arthur had them, always in use of course, like the pipes of Pan. Social principles, interests. Everything he touched," she said, "turned to gold." She noticed that the people in the room were thinning out. "And everything I lay my fingers on," she said in irritation, "goes dim."

She looked around the salon, at backs and faces. Something was surely demanded of her somewhere: some one of importance overlooked, the cigarettes run out, her mother-in-law expiring, in the thick of nobles, for a cup of tea.

"The most moral man," she said. "I don't know how well you know him." The room was waltzing, swooning before her eyes. "I'm in such a pocket," said the Contessa bitterly to the young man beside her. Her hand suddenly pressed fiercely on his arm. "If Arthur sent you—particularly, I mean," she said, "for the love of God tell me."

The young man sat still in his chair.

"I'm—I'm so sorry," he said in a moment. The little chain on his wrist was set to ringing like a bell. "I know he admires—he admires your courage."

"My courage!" said the Contessa with a laugh.

"Your courage in facing the same people, the same conversation, every day of your life the same faces—"

"The same tea," went on the Contessa as she lit another cigarette. "I must remember to have orange pekoe tomorrow. Is that all he said?"

The young man looked at the Contessa helplessly.

"I'm in such a pocket," said the Contessa weakly in a moment. She felt her courage slipping from under. "I've been such a fool," she said. "Everything I touch turns black."

"Even a title?" said the new young man.

"My God," said the Contessa. "What can you do to keep things from tarnishing? What can you do?" She ran her tongue over her lips as though they were parched for water. "Is Arthur a happy man?" she said. Her eyes could have cut the truth from his heart. "Tell me how it is," she said to his silence. "Arthur has never married. Sometimes it comes into my head that maybe he himself is grieving."

"I don't think Arthur is interested in marriage," said the new young man in confusion. "I don't think he was ever very much interested in women that way, you know." He played with the little bangle on his arm and looked away from her.

What a Scotchman, thought the Contessa! With his mouth buttoned up tight, not a word of intelligence to dole out to her, hoarding his cheese parings and candle shavings! She could have shaken in her two hands the ignorant common little man who sat by her side. Perhaps he had been up with Arthur at Queen's, and that's all there was to their friendship. Maybe he hadn't seen Arthur for a century, except casually passing him on the street, and Arthur remembering and being decent to the insignificant little squirt who had sat beside him, or before, or behind him in college.

"How long is it," she said as she blew the smoke out through her nose, "since you've seen Arthur?"

"He came to see me off at the boat the day I left," said

the new young man. "He said I was to see if you were still
as beautiful as you had always been."

"And what shall you say?" said the Contessa. She
looked at him so closely that, for all her beauty, there was
nothing gentle left in her face. Why couldn't he speak,
what was he keeping back from her? He, with his precious
little ways, she knew him for what he was.

"I don't know what you were like before," said the
young man smiling.

"No," said the Contessa. "Well, I am not the same. I
was a foolish young woman. One minute I made a fool of
myself over Arthur, and the next I wouldn't have him
under my roof. You've no idea how it was. He took me
home after a dance one night," said the Contessa, "a
shindy. We'd known each other for years then, and you
may know him well, but he probably never told you that.
And every one was away, so he put me to bed like a
mother, tucked the covers under my chin, and brushed my
hair out on the pillow for half an hour. I had so much
punch in me that it was turning cartwheels in my head.
What do you think of that?" said the Contessa. "I slept
the night with him on the floor beside me. When I woke up
in the morning he was lying flat on his back on the rug
with his legs crossed smoking and reading poetry."

The Contessa's hand was so agitated that she put it out
of sight under the tea table.

"Now, what do you think of that?" she said with a cry of
laughter.

She was at the end of her patience, the extremity, the
last fringe of it was disappearing, slowly, like the hem of a
skirt up the stair. Dull as a ditch he was, with no flicker of
light in him. A frail little chap dressed up like a parrot.

What, what in the name of all the saints had Arthur in common with him? There was something in him as stupid and breakable as a doll.

"Do you see Arthur very much, very often?" she said in desperation to him.

"Oh, rather," said the young man. She thought there was something dry and evil in the quality of his skin. "We room together," he said.

The Contessa looked at him at length.

"Oh, you do, do you?" she said in a moment.

She didn't know where it belonged. She couldn't make it fit. Desperate for company poor Arthur must be: black, abandoned, lost forever to love. She could fancy him getting up in the morning, slamming the door on this jackanapes in irritation. Arthur, glowering all the time now, of course, with never an arrow of Irish wit flying. Perhaps the lease will expire soon, thought the Contessa, and Arthur will be rid of him. How he must writhe!

"Love—" she began suddenly. And then she stopped short. She couldn't possibly speak like that before this dandiprat!

"Yes," said the new young man as though he knew very well. He smoothed the side of his hand in conceit over his shining hair.

"When one is as young as a colt," said the Contessa.

"Oh, of course," said the new young man. For a minute she thought he seemed to be accepting an apology from her. "One is pure," he said. "One understands nothing."

"Isn't it funny?" said the Contessa. She was thinking of Arthur's shy honor. Honor, my eye, she used to say to him with her tongue as sharp as God knows what. "I'd know how to manage him today," she said grimly.

"Oh, I daresay!" said the new young man. But his tone did not convince her. In spite of the heat of the afternoon, he was pulling on his gloves to go.

HIS IDEA OF A MOTHER

The road wound straight on, with a small branch to the left, and there seemed no reason at all to turn and cross the stream that slid along on the other side. A queer thought it would be indeed to follow the cattle path up over the hill.

But the little boy was on his way home from school one day, when he stopped at Drury's Crossing and looked up at the signpost that was insisting that the branch to the left led to Shopton, and the road before him to something else again. It came into his head that the path and the way it was going had been left unmentioned. He sat down there to have a good look at the hill that was stretching away beyond.

Across the stream there seemed to be a great amount of soft, sweet turf, and of greenness spread out all over. Higher, there were trees springing up, as lyrical as dancing women, though all he could see in them was the way they moved in the wind. Beside the stream there was a willow or two drying out its hair.

The path did not quite make the grade to the castle of trees that was bowing this way and that at the top. Just a

minute before it got there, it threw up its two small white
arms in despair and was lost forever in the blowing weeds.
The little boy sat looking at what lay before him, and
calling upon the courage that would take him over the
fence and the stream and up the hill.

The whole of the hill itself was spotted with islands of
dung, and if he had summoned any courage at all, it
perished at the sight of a cow making her way down. He
thought she must be on her way down to drink, but when
she spied him, she stood quite still and looked at him with
her soft dim eyes. He sat hard and small against the fence,
wondering if she had any young ones behind her and
watching her full sagging throat and the gentle shifting of
her jaw. Presently, another great angular cow followed the
first one, and then another, and before the little boy could
get to his feet and move away, at least eight of the beasts
were stumbling down the stony path.

He stood for a while in the road, watching them lower
their muzzles to drink at the water, and the bright beads
from the stream that gathered on their sparse beards, and
the long ribbons of slobber that hung from the ends of
their mouths. Every time they flung wide their rosy
nostrils to drink, he could see the clear ripples which their
breath tossed across the surface of the water. He had no
great feeling of pride for himself as he stood on the other
side of the fence from them, for if men and their courage
were strangers to him, at least he knew that the delicate
thing which the sight of big animals set shaking between
his ribs was fragile enough to be the ornament of any little
girl. His father had been dead eight years, and what he
was like he had no idea at all.

His idea of a mother was something else again. How

long she had been dead, he did not know. He was thinking of her as he walked backward up the road. His dragging feet were startling up fine clouds of dust in the roadway, and in the soles of them was more than languor, as if he did not care whether he ever found his way back to her or not. "Aunt Petoo, skee-doo," he thought. He looked at the cows, and watched their tails moving venomously across their bony rumps. "Aunt Petoo, skee-doo."

He found her squatting down in the garden before the house. She had a trowel in her hand and she was prodding at her flowers. She looked up at him and pushed her straw bonnet off her brow with the back of her hand.

"Did ye ever take a walk up the path over the hill at Drury's Crossing?" he said to her, as he swung on the gate.

She shook her head absently.

"Will you get me some water in the can, there you are," was what she said.

The little boy set down his books.

"Don't set your books down there," she said. "Why do you have to swing on the gate every time you come in like that?"

"Did ye ever take a walk on that path over the hill at Drury's Crossing?" asked the little boy.

"Will you get me some water in the can?" said Aunt Petoo.

The little boy walked off with the can in his hand. He was looking around about him, and up, and over, and looking at the house in its vines, and the trees waving and the birds flying over his shoulder, and in this way he tripped on a croquet wicket and fell down.

"Get up," said Reynolds.

The little boy sat rubbing his shins and looking sourly

at the toes of Reynolds' boots. Reynolds was the only man
he had ever known intimately. His vest was black and
yellow, and it was his place to ride behind Aunt Petoo's
horses and to mow the grass. He could drown kittens,
dispose of rabbits with one whack of the hand, and he
could swim. In the summer, he could swim the river with
the muscles of his breasts swelling and gathering like
snowballs in the water. As he stood above the little boy on
the croquet lawn, he was red with anger. In one hand he
held a carriage whip, and in the other an urchin.

"Look here at this urchin!" he said in contempt to Aunt
Petoo. "He was come across stealing cherries!"

There in the sun shone the flushed and dripping face,
the contorted mouth, and the terror of the urchin boy. The
little boy himself began to whimper at the sight. When he
lifted his hand to wipe off his own tears with the back of it,
he could see it was shaking as if in the very teeth of
cowardice.

"What are you going to do with the urchin?" said the
little boy. He whispered it in terror across the grass.

"Thrash him," said Reynolds. "It's what his own father
ought to be giving him, not me!" Reynolds swung about
to the old lady. "I'm going to thrash him proper, Miss
Petoo," he said. He held the urchin up in the sun.

"Not here," said Aunt Petoo. "The wretches squawk
so." With the greatest precision she pinched off the leaves
that sprang up along the stalk of a begonia. Her mouth
did not relent. "Take him around by the stable," she said.
"The slugs got into the very best strawberries last night.
Not a sizeable one for tea, Reynolds!"

"Aunt Petoo," said the little boy, "don't let him thrash
the urchin."

Aunt Petoo looked up from the flowers. The little boy was standing beside her.

"Don't, don't, ah, please, don't, Aunt Petoo!"

He spoke very quietly, and the "ah" seemed a strange sound for such a small boy to be making. It was a church, a poetry sound, and to hear him using it for a moment put her out.

"But a thief," she said. "A thief who steals . . ."

The little boy's face was shaking like a small fist in her face.

"Aunt Petoo, Aunt Petoo," he said. "Please, please, ah, please, please, don't let him do it!"

The garden was as soft and melting as an all-day sucker between the teeth. Aunt Petoo cracked off a great bite of it.

"Oh, skee-doo," she said. "Get along with you! Let Reynolds go his own way and you get about yours! I've been after you for water in the can . . ."

The little boy flung himself against her knees.

"Ah, Aunt Petoo, Aunt Petoo," he cried. "No, no, no, no, Aunt Petoo! Let the urchin go once this time, ah, ah, ah, ah, ah, Aunt Petoo!"

A terrible look of venom crossed Aunt Petoo's face. He had made the garden go sick on her very tongue. Reynolds had walked off with the urchin under his arm, and the little boy lay on the ground at her feet, biting fiercely at the turf.

"Now listen here," she said. She shook at his shoulder. "Your Uncle Dan is coming home. What do you think of a soldier hearing all this crying and this screaming?" Her voice would never give in. "It's a shame for a boy and no soldier would bear it."

The little boy lay still.

"Who is my Uncle Dan?" he said, without lifting his head.

"Your father's brother," said Aunt Petoo. "With long whiskers and a sword."

The day had begun to fade away when the little boy started off down the road. That his father's brother was coming back was the thought that remained in his mind. He thought of this until every tree he passed became a menace to him, and his shoelace untied and tapping at his ankle made him skid with terror in the gloom.

When he came to Drury's Crossing, he slipped with the greatest glibness beneath the bars of the fence and leapt across the stream. His blood was singing like a harp and he was not afraid at all. As he ran, he startled a little group of cottontails across the path. He stopped and watched them scampering off through the impenetrable grass. The water was shining like a mirror far below him, and the willows looked as soft and airy as feathers blowing along the stream.

Milkweed pods were tapping at the cups of his knees, and now and again the wing of a moth caressed his cheek. The sight of a moth in the room with him made his spine crawl, but here in the dark it was natural and left him with no fear at all. When he seated himself in the deep grass, he felt as if he were crouching on the hearth close before the fire. Even the wind that rose was as warm as a scarf around his neck.

Whether he fell asleep then, or whether his eyes were open all the time, he did not know. But however it was, he had not been sitting there long when he saw the cows beginning to loom out of the darkness and make their way down towards the stream. They were going slowly down, with their heads hanging like heavy copper bells between their forelegs, their jaws endlessly and softly crunching, and when they stopped at all, it was to lift their heads and call softly out through the falling night.

The deep mellow sound of the cows calling to one another was so beautiful that the little boy tried the sound of it in his own throat. He lifted his head to catch the soft shape of the cows' mouths and the turn of their velvet tongues in their jaws. His nostrils were stretched wide open, imitating the cows' rosy nostrils, which were spread full as harvest moons.

The great dark beasts seemed in no great haste to descend the hill and they loitered here and there in the rich night. Had they been horses, thought the little boy, the least sound of him stirring would have sent them off in alarm, but here were the cows cropping at the grass and munching it almost at his feet, as though the smell of him there meant nothing to them. Any movement he made seemed natural to them, and when he put out his hand and stroked the foreleg of one cow that stood nearby, she lifted her head in no dismay whatever and snuffed deeply at his neck. Such a blast of sweet meadowy odor passed across his face that he shuddered with delight.

It was then that the beast he had stroked bent her knees under her and lay down in the grass. He could not perceive her in the darkness, but from the sound and breath of her, and the soft swing and crunch of her jaws, he knew that she had folded her gray horny hoofs under her heart and was chewing gently there beside him in the grass. When he moved closer, she made no sign. Even the touch of his hand on her strong shoulder did not cause her to stir. When he stroked the stiff, sleek curve of her ear in his open hand, she flicked it solemnly back and forth.

The little boy shifted himself against her and pressed his small lean back into her strong covered bones. The endless rhythm of her cud swung easily through all her rich shoulder and bosom. Great tough ribbons of movement ran strongly through her flesh. The little boy had laid his face against her neck, and there was his ear stroked and soothed with it. He could hear the soft humming of her belly as it greeted and returned the food from her fruitful jaws. On the ground he could feel the feast of white violets and clover heads that had been spread there before her. As he lay against her he thought of the great full sack of milk that was hanging between her legs.

He was thinking what a comfort it was to have the warm body of the cow against him in the field, and while he was drowsing, suddenly she whipped her head about so violently that she gave him a fierce blow in the ribs with the side of her horn. When he had found his senses again, he thought it must have been a fly that had disturbed her or else she would never have struck him with such force. This was the thought that was in his head when she turned again towards him and rubbed her great bony face against his arm. Such blasts did she thrust from her nose on him, like a mother cat smelling out her young, that he thought he would be blown down the black field. But presently, when she had snuffed in enough of him, her tongue began to move rudely across his hand, lifting his fingers up and turning them over as if they were so many stalks of clover. When she had done with his hands, she licked her way up the coarse stuff of his jacket and there was his neck and his ear and all the hairs on his head getting such a scrubbing and such a loving as would have taken his hide off had it been anyone else that was doing it to him.

It was when the half-moon was coming up from behind the trees that the mother cow, without any kind of warning at all, suddenly straightened out her legs and stood up in the grass. A terrible feeling of despair pierced the little boy's heart. But she went ambling quietly off, with her tail swinging, and the little boy himself started reluctantly down the hill. The whole world was returning again under the illumination of the moon. The trees were uncurling out of the darkness, and the grass was moving like a sea. When the little boy reached the water, he stopped for a moment. In the middle of the stream lay a little broken moon, rippling back and forth. He knelt down and put his two hands about its moving edges and tried to lift it up. In a moment the little moon was rippling back and forth again and his hands were wet and cold.

The little boy crossed the fence and started up the dusty road. The old landmarks were familiar to him in the strange light. When he came to the gate of the garden, some kind of human fear possessed him. It was a surprise to himself when he pushed the gate open and walked up the path. A man, with a pipe in his mouth, was turning up and down the terrace. The little boy stood still for a while and watched this sight. When the man turned again he looked down the garden, and he too stopped in his walk.

"Hullo," he remarked. He had no whiskers.

"Are you Uncle Dan?" said the little boy.

"Right you are," said the man.

"Are you going to thrash me?" said the little boy.

"Is that customary in greeting a nephew?" asked Uncle Dan.

"I ran away," explained the little boy. "If my father was here, he'd thrash me—"

"Hold on, sir," said Uncle Dan.

The little boy stood staring at him in silence. Uncle Dan glanced over his shoulder.

"I say," he remarked in a lower tone, "shall we walk down the road a bit so we shan't be disturbed?"

THE REVIVED MODERN CLASSICS

H. E. Bates
A Month by the Lake & Other Stories. Introduction by Anthony Burgess. Seventeen "nearly perfect stories" *(Publishers Weekly)* by the English master (1905-1974)—"...without an equal in England in the kind of story he made his own."—*London Times.* Cloth & ND Paperbook 645.   (In preparation: *A Party for the Girls: Six Stories)*

Mikhail Bulgakov
The Life of Monsieur de Molière. Trans. by Mirra Ginsburg. A vivid portrait of the great French 17th-century satirist by one of the great Russian satirists of our own century. Cloth & NDP 601

Joyce Cary
"Second Trilogy": *Prisoner of Grace. Except the Lord. Not Honour More.* "Even better than Cary's 'First Trilogy,' this is one of the great political novels of this century."—*San Francisco Examiner.* NDP606, 607, & 608. *A House of Children.* Reprint of the delightful autobiographical novel. NDP631

Maurice Collis
The Land of the Great Image. "...a vivid and illuminating study written with the care and penetration that an artist as well as a historian must exercise to make the exotic past live and breathe for us."—Eudora Welty. NDP612

Ronald Firbank
Three More Novels. "...these novels are an inexhaustible source of pleasure."—*The Village Voice Literary Supplement.* NDP614

Romain Gary
The Life Before Us (Madame Rosa). Written under the pseudonym of Émile Ajar. Trans. by Ralph Manheim. "You won't forget Momo and Madame Rosa when you close the book. 'The Life Before Us' is a moving reading experience, if you don't mind a good cry." — *St. Louis Post-Dispatch*. NDP604. *Promise at Dawn*. A memoir "bursting with life... Gary's art has been to combine the comic and the tragic." — *The New Yorker*. NDP635

Henry Green
Back. "...a rich, touching story, flecked all over by Mr. Green's intuition of the concealed originality of ordinary human beings." — V. S. Pritchett. NDP517

Siegfried Lenz
The German Lesson. Trans. by Ernst Kaiser and Eithne Wilkins. "A book of rare depth and brilliance..." — *The New York Times*. NDP618

Henri Michaux
A Barbarian in Asia. Trans. by Sylvia Beach. "It is superb in its swift illuminations and its wit..." — Alfred Kazin, *The New Yorker*. NDP622

Kenneth Rexroth
Classics Revisited. Sixty brief, radiant essays on the books Rexroth called the "basic documents in the history of the imagination." NDP621

Raymond Queneau
The Blue Flowers. Trans. by Barbara Wright. "...an exuberant meditation on the novel, narrative conventions, and readers." — *The Washington Post*. NDP595

Robert Penn Warren
At Heaven's Gate. A novel of power and corruption in the deep South of the 1920s. NDP588